"You've been coo[...]
time to introduce y[...] [...]e
winked at Steven.

"That's why I'm here," Steven said as he gulped down the rest of his beer. "My whole life I've been Mr. Responsibility. Now it's time I started having fun."

"Well, you've come to the right guy to show you how to do that," Mike said as a fiery redhead walked by and threw her arms around him, planting a big, wet kiss on his cheek.

"You've got it made," Steven said, wide-eyed. "Beautiful babes. Not caring about anyone else but yourself. That's the life for me. You can have a different woman every night." Steven shrugged. "I only wish that were my life. Then I wouldn't have to get all torn up inside about just one woman."

Bantam Books in the Sweet Valley University series
Ask your bookseller for the books you have missed

And don't miss these
Sweet Valley University Thriller Editions:

SWEET VALLEY UNIVERSITY®

Here Comes the Bride

Written by
Laurie John

Created by
FRANCINE PASCAL

BANTAM BOOKS
NEW YORK · TORONTO · LONDON · SYDNEY · AUCKLAND

RL 6, age 12 and up

HERE COMES THE BRIDE
A Bantam Book / April 1996

Sweet Valley High® and Sweet Valley University®
are registered trademarks of Francine Pascal
Conceived by Francine Pascal
Produced by Daniel Weiss Associates, Inc.
33 West 17th Street
New York, NY 10011

ISBN: 0-553-56702-0

Published simultaneously in the United States and Canada

Bantam Books are published by Bantam Books, a division of Bantam
Doubleday Dell Publishing Group, Inc. Its trademark, consisting of the
words "Bantam Books" and the portrayal of a rooster, is Registered in
U.S. Patent and Trademark Office and in other countries. Marca
Registrada. Bantam Books, 1540 Broadway, New York, New York 10036.

PRINTED IN THE UNITED STATES OF AMERICA

OPM   0 9 8 7 6 5 4 3 2 1

To Bari Paige Rosenow

Chapter One

Billie Winkler knelt over the back of the dark green corduroy sofa in her living room. She looked down at the sunlit street for what seemed like the hundredth time in the last hour.

"Where *are* you, Steven Wakefield?" she whispered nervously, sinking down onto the sofa and hugging her knees to her chest. She brushed a strand of dark brown hair from her worried forehead. Just because she and Steven had broken up didn't mean she couldn't be concerned about him, did it?

Last night she'd seen him ride off with Mike McAllery. Now it was nearly nine in the morning, and they still weren't back. She strained her ears, hoping to hear the low rumble of Mike's motorcycle.

Billie knew that staying out all night was normal behavior for Mike. But it wasn't for Steven. At least it hadn't been, before Steven had moved out of the

1

apartment he and Billie had been sharing for the last year and into Mike's bachelor pad.

Rising from the sofa, Billie turned to face the long wood-framed mirror on the far wall of the living room. The image that stared back at her was a pale, ghostly version of the Billie Winkler she'd always known. Her dark blue eyes, normally sparkling, were dull and swollen from days of crying. Her mouth was frozen in a grim line. Even her shiny brown hair seemed to have lost its sheen. And the clothes she was wearing, an old T-shirt and jeans, looked grubby and creased.

She knew her exhausted appearance wasn't entirely due to her and Steven's breakup. Her body had been on as much of a roller-coaster ride as her emotions.

"One week ago, Billie Winkler," she reminded her petite reflection, "you were a pregnant woman about to be married." She felt the lump she'd been carrying around in her throat for the past week grow two sizes.

The pregnancy had been unexpected, unplanned for, and, she had to admit, unwanted. The surprise news had thrown her and Steven into a state of total confusion. Suddenly every decision they made had lifelong consequences. To have the baby or not. To get married or not. Even after they'd decided to do both those things, there had been doubts.

"It wasn't fair," Billie told the anguished eyes that stared back at her from the mirror. "I was too young for marriage and a baby." Plus, she'd had her music to think about. Billie had just won a scholarship to study guitar in Spain. Steven, of course, had assumed she'd give up her music career and devote herself to being a wife and mother. *And a corporate attorney,* she reminded herself. Steven had never been supportive of her guitar playing, and things had only gotten worse once she'd become pregnant.

Billie turned away from the mirror and her worn-out reflection. The memory of the past weeks sent an involuntary shudder through her body. She and Steven had been practically at each other's throats. *Of course we were fighting,* she thought. *Who wouldn't argue under those circumstances?*

But that last fight had been the worst.

They'd finally agreed to get married. Steven's mother had been busy with the arrangements, calling in the caterers and the florist. Steven's sister, Jessica, had her fashion company designing the dresses that Jessica and her twin, Elizabeth, would wear as maids of honor. Billie had felt like a backseat rider in a speeding car. Things were happening way too fast and she'd lost all control.

She'd blown up at Steven and he'd blown up back. Hard. He'd made it clear he wasn't happy about rushing into marriage and parenthood either. But he was prepared to do his duty. Then came the terrible pain in her abdomen and the miscarriage. After that there hadn't seemed to be much reason to get married anymore.

"Not even much of a reason to stay together," Billie sobbed to the empty room. She buried her face in her hands, hot tears running down her cheeks. *I miss him so much,* she thought.

The sound of Mike's motorcycle drew her back to the living-room window. She sniffed back her tears, breathing a sigh of relief as she watched the tall, lanky frame of her ex-fiancé hop off the back of Mike's bike. She'd know those broad shoulders and long legs anywhere. Billie glanced at the old-style diner clock on the wall. Now it was close to ten in the morning, which meant Steven was missing Business Law, his most important class.

Billie reluctantly tore her eyes from the window. "What Steven does now is none of your business," she reminded herself, fighting the ache that was again rising in her chest. But staying out all night on a motorcycle? Billie couldn't count the number of times Steven had complained about his sister, Jessica, riding on the back of Mike's bike. *Couldn't he and Mike at least have taken Mike's vintage car?* Billie thought. She glanced at the space where the bright red Mustang was usually parked and realized she hadn't seen it for a couple of weeks.

"Apparently Steven isn't the man you once knew." Billie sighed to herself. But then, a lot of things had changed. It hadn't been that long ago that Jessica and Mike were married and Mike was Steven's sworn enemy. Now Jessica and Mike's marriage had been annulled and Steven and Mike were practically best friends.

There was a knock at the door and Billie jumped. *Could it be Steven?* She rushed to the door and flung it open only to find the sweet, matching smiles of Steven's twin sisters, Elizabeth and Jessica Wakefield, greeting her.

"Hi, Billie," the twins chimed in unison.

"Hey, come in," Billie offered. She let a smile hide her disappointment.

4

Jessica, wearing a short turquoise dress that ignited her blue-green eyes, strode through the door. Her long blond hair was loose, but swept back off her forehead. "We came over to see how you were doing." She collapsed on the living-room couch and picked up a copy of *Vogue* from the coffee table.

Elizabeth gave Billie a big hug as she stepped inside. "And to see if there was anything we could do for you," she added, giving Jessica a stern look. Elizabeth wore jeans and a white tailored blouse. Her golden hair was pulled back in a high, bouncing ponytail. Wisps of blond hair that had fallen out of her ponytail fringed her luminous eyes.

"Thanks, but I'm fine, really," Billie said, starting for the kitchen. "Can I get anyone a drink?"

Jessica and Elizabeth followed her.

"An iced cappuccino would be great," Jessica said, brightly perching on the kitchen counter.

Elizabeth yanked her sister down, her aquamarine eyes flashing. "Anything you're having is fine, Billie, but you sit—we'll get it."

"There's coffee on the stove," Billie said, smiling to herself and taking a seat at the kitchen table. That was just like the twins—Jessica bouncing in, asking for the world, and Elizabeth ever so conscious of other people's feelings. Billie realized with a pang how much she'd come to care for both sisters as if they were her own.

Elizabeth poured them each a cup of coffee, and Jessica got a container of milk from the refrigerator.

"So," Billie began when they were all settled around the table. "How is everyone?"

"Ummm . . . uh, fine," Elizabeth stuttered.

"Everything is . . . fine." Suddenly Elizabeth's attention was focused on the glass jars of pasta that lined the countertops.

Billie turned to Jessica, who hesitated, her bright eyes darting around the room.

"Sugar, anyone?" Jessica asked nervously.

The refrigerator hummed loudly in the uncomfortable silence that followed. Billie sighed. The big topic, her and Steven's breakup, was hovering above them like a dark cloud. She could see the twins were trying to avoid talking about their brother.

Billie reached for her coffee and took a sip. "Okay, you guys. How's Steven?" The twins giggled and seemed to relax in their chairs now that the subject was out in the open.

Elizabeth gave a small smile. "Actually, I don't know how Steven is. He seems okay, as far as I can tell, but I haven't seen much of him lately."

Jessica took a sip of her coffee and then stirred in a sugar cube. "I saw him yesterday, but he was in a hurry. He said hello, good-bye, and that was it."

"Was he sad or upset?" Billie asked, biting her lower lip. She couldn't stand to imagine Steven unhappy. But what if he was happy? Wouldn't that be even worse?

Jessica shook her head. "I couldn't tell; it was so quick. But he isn't sharing whatever he's going through with me."

Elizabeth got up and poured herself some more coffee. "Or me," she added. "But I'm sure he'll come around soon. You know Steven."

I used to think I did, Billie thought. But since

he'd moved out, she didn't seem to know him at all.

"Well, I've got to talk to him," Jessica said, standing up and running her slender fingers through her silky hair. "I think I'll stick my head in upstairs. First I've got to check my makeup."

Billie caught Elizabeth's eye, and they exchanged knowing smiles. Was Jessica's primping just business as usual? Billie wondered. Or was it because Steven was now staying with Mike, Jessica's ex-husband?

Jessica flipped open her compact mirror just outside Mike's front door and took one last look. "What a difference a little makeup makes," she said to herself.

She and her twin sister, Elizabeth, would be considered beautiful in any case with their heart-shaped faces and tall, slim, athletic bodies. And on the days when Jessica went for the natural look, she had to admit they were hard to tell apart. But with a few strokes of blush here, a little coral tint on her lips there, she and Elizabeth could hardly be called identical anymore. She was clearly the more beautiful one.

It's true, Jessica thought, snapping her compact closed and slipping it into her handbag, *people are always noticing me*. She pushed away the thought that maybe it was because she was always getting into trouble.

No, it was simple. She lived at a higher intensity level than other people. Even more so than her twin. Jessica loved her sister dearly, but they couldn't be more different.

Elizabeth didn't seem to mind the drudgery of life. Going to classes, studying for tests, even doing all that investigative work for her news stories for WSVU, the Sweet Valley University television station.

Not for me, Jessica thought. *Why investigate the news if you can* be *the news? And why do all the legwork if you have a chance to skip to the head of the class?* Though why Elizabeth always seemed to have steady boyfriends while Jessica went from one man disaster to another she didn't know.

Jessica pressed her lips together one last time to ensure perfect lipstick distribution and softly tapped at Mike's front door. A shiver of anticipation ran down her spine as the door slowly opened. She felt her knees begin to buckle as the rugged good looks of her ex-husband stared back at her. Even in an old flannel shirt and faded jeans, with his dark, tousled hair falling messily over his forehead, Mike was a total hunk.

"I'm here to see Steven," Jessica announced, pulling her eyes away from his and starting through the doorway.

"Oh?" Mike taunted, casually blocking the way with one of his powerful arms. "Looking extra beautiful, and it's not for me?"

Jessica ducked under his arm, her face heating up. Next time she'd show him and wear an old T-shirt and ripped-up jeans. And she knew just the ones. She smiled wryly to herself. They were faded blue and hugged every curve of her body.

"Steven," Mike called out, "your little sister is here."

Jessica's eyes flashed angrily at the insolent grin

8

that was stretched across Mike's face. "I wasn't so little when we were married."

"No." Mike snorted derisively, crossing his muscular arms and leaning against the wall. "You're one of those rare people who gets more immature over time."

Jessica's mouth dropped open, but she quickly closed it. She was here to see Steven. She wasn't going to let Mike McAllery get her all riled up this time.

Bruce Patman followed the curvaceous line of his girlfriend Lila Fowler's legs. He was stooped over, peering through the crack below the drawn shade that covered the window of Lila's Doughnuts. Lila had pulled the shade down on him right after locking him out of the store. And all over a simple misunderstanding.

Sure, he'd walked out on her when her business was falling to pieces, with bills pouring in and that scam artist Clyde Pelmer threatening to sue over a fake accident. Bruce grimaced. *Okay, a not-so-simple misunderstanding,* he thought. *More like a clear case of Benedict Arnold-itis.* But that didn't mean he wanted to break up.

He took one last look at her legs before straightening his back. "It was those legs that got me into all this trouble in the first place," he mused. "If it hadn't been for those legs driving me crazy while we were stranded in the Sierra Nevada, I never would have noticed what a knockout she is."

Bruce shook his head in amazement. Sometimes it was still hard to believe that they were going out.

He and Lila had squabbled since childhood and probably would have continued until old age. But after Bruce had crashed his new two-seater plane while giving Lila a "lift" to a Theta dinner dance, they'd survived a harrowing week in the frozen wilderness together. If it hadn't been for Lila, he might not be alive right now. She wasn't the stuck-up brat he'd always known but a coolheaded, competent, brave woman.

Bruce sheepishly kicked a pebble on the sidewalk. "Okay, I admit it," he shouted to the closed-up storefront. "I was wrong. But I was the one who bought you Lila's Doughnuts in the first place when you were searching for a purpose in life."

Two elderly ladies heading toward him clutched each other and crossed the street to avoid him. He must have been quite a sight—a lunatic yelling at a closed door.

Bruce sighed. It was also true, he had to admit, that Lila had turned Lila's Doughnuts into a really chic hangout for the socially aware, with all profits going to the Sweet Valley Coalition for Battered Women. She'd also managed to pull herself out of her financial troubles without any help from him. So why couldn't she forgive him now?

Bruce rattled the locked front door. Lila was in there with her lawyer, drawing up a contract to permanently turn the property over to a nonprofit organization. As far as Bruce could tell she wouldn't make a dime, but if she played her cards right, it could be a great tax write-off. Bruce rattled the door again. He should be in there with her.

"What?" Lila snapped, flinging open the door.

10

The angry pink of her cheeks was almost a perfect match for the sleeveless magenta jumper she was wearing. "What do you want? Can't you see I'm busy with my lawyer?"

"It's all right," the lawyer said, coming to the door. "Talk to your young man. I need to make a few phone calls. I'll be in my Mercedes."

Lila flashed her beautiful dark brown eyes at Bruce. Eyes that could take him to the moon or just as easily send him crashing down to earth.

"I wanted to see if you need some help." He gulped.

"From you?" Lila scoffed, poking him in the chest. "Mr. I'm-Bailing-Out-When-the-Going-Gets-Tough?"

Bruce threw up his hands in mock surrender. "I'm sorry."

"For what?" Lila narrowed her eyes warily.

"For not being there when you needed me," Bruce said in his most contrite voice.

Lila crossed her slender arms and leaned against the door. "And?" she prompted.

"For letting you down and being a jerk."

"Just a jerk?" Lila asked, arching one perfectly shaped eyebrow.

"Come on, Lila," Bruce said. Apologizing was hard enough as it was.

"Just a jerk?" Lila asked again, more forcefully this time.

She wasn't going to let him off the hook, that was obvious. "For being a first-class, major, thoughtless jerk," Bruce said as fast as he could. "Now, please, Lila, forgive me. I'm miserable without you."

11

"Really?" Her mouth softened into a smile.

"Really," Bruce said. Each of them took a step closer. He reached out, hugging her tight in the doorway, and they lost themselves in a deep, passionate kiss.

A loud "ahem" brought Bruce and Lila back to their senses. On the pavement in front of them stood a suave-looking man in a charcoal gray suit and red power tie.

I wonder how he manages to conceal his dorsal fin? Bruce smirked. *Because he's a shark if I ever saw one.*

"I'm Mr. Petty," the man said, holding out his business card. "I represent Fowler Enterprises. A small, family-run business looking to purchase a modest lot for a modest price. Do you happen to know who owns this property?"

Bruce stifled a laugh. The shark wasn't so sharp after all. Obviously he didn't know he was talking to the daughter of Robert Fowler, chairman and CEO of Fowler Enterprises. And that business about Fowler Enterprises being a small, family-run operation. What a joke! Fowler Enterprises was one of the biggest syndicates in all of California and the most cutthroat by far. They were planning to build a luxury apartment complex and had been buying up lots all over the area. If they were looking to buy the property Lila's Doughnuts was on, that meant it was worth a ton of money.

Bruce looked over at Lila, hoping she was taking it all in. He watched with amusement as she smiled and took the man's card. "The owner is temporarily unavailable," Lila said sweetly. "But I'll make sure this card gets into the right hands."

12

"Thank you," Mr. Petty said with a small bow. "Mr. Fowler is particularly interested in concluding this business quickly."

"No problem," Lila said. "Thank you for stopping by." The man walked away as Lila stepped back into the shop. She pulled Bruce in after her and closed the door, giggling.

"Did you see those fangs?" Bruce asked.

Lila grinned. "I think I'll tell my lawyer I want to hold off on turning this property over to charity." She rubbed her hands together. "I'd like to see what Daddy has in mind."

"Good idea," Bruce said as Lila's softly parted lips again met his. It wasn't just the shape of Lila's legs. He liked the way her mind worked, too.

Steven rose unsteadily from the narrow cot in Mike's cluttered guest room. He gingerly stepped over the stacks of old car and motorcycle magazines that littered the bare floor. His sister Jessica's indignant voice was ringing through the apartment. He knew he'd have to get out to the living room and run interference between Jessica and Mike if he ever wanted to sleep. And after another night on the town with Mike, sleep was something Steven desperately needed. He lurched toward the door, nearly tripping over a mound of dirty clothes.

"What's up, Jess?" Steven asked, propping himself up in the doorway. His head was pounding and his mouth felt as if he'd been eating wool socks.

Jessica pushed back a strand of her hair, causing her bangle bracelets to tinkle. The sound echoed in Steven's aching head like cannon fire.

13

"Jess," he said, putting up his hand. "Don't make any sudden movements."

Jessica placed her hands on her hips. "What's wrong with you?"

Mike chuckled. "It's called a hangover. I'll fix you a Bloody Mary, buddy."

"No," Steven moaned. He'd already vowed never to drink again. "I'm all right."

"Okay," Mike said. "Ginger ale. Next best thing for the morning after." He disappeared into the kitchen.

Steven turned to Jessica and motioned to Mike's black leather couch. "Just take a seat and don't talk too loud." He eased his exhausted body into the chrome-and-leather wing chair on the other side of the coffee table, grateful to be off his aching feet.

Jessica dropped down onto the couch, letting her heavy handbag fall to the floor with a loud thud.

Steven bit his lip to keep from crying out.

His sister's blue-green eyes narrowed unsympathetically. "It's about Val and me," she started. "I'm not sure what to do. Our fashion show was such a huge success that Val got an offer to work in L.A."

Val Tripler was a hip, stylish young woman who Jessica had met while working at Taylor's department store. They'd gone into business together— Val designing trendy silk wrap skirts and blouses and Jessica acting as company sales rep. Steven knew all about this, but he was having a hard time concentrating. His eyes started to close.

"Steven," Jessica's voice snapped him back, "are you listening?"

Steven slowly nodded.

"Anyway," she went on, "Val said if I wanted, she'd turn down the job and stay in business with me. But I don't know. Maybe it would be smarter to cash out now and concentrate on school."

Steven shrugged. "Why don't you sleep on it?"

"Steven!" Jessica yelled. "It's practically eleven o'clock in the morning. I've done my sleeping."

Steven grabbed his head to keep it from splitting in two. "I was just trying to help," he mumbled.

"You'd be more help," Jessica continued, pulling her dark leather bag onto her lap and extracting a large notepad, "if you'd look over these numbers."

Steven feebly accepted the pad that Jessica handed him and looked down at the endless rows of figures. His eyes could barely focus. "I can't look at this."

"Why not?" Jessica shrieked. "You *are* taking a class in business law. Or at least you *were* until you moved in with Mike."

Steven closed his eyes to make the numbers stop swimming, but nothing could drown out his sister's shrillness except distance. "Later, Jess," he said with a groan, getting up and stumbling back to his bedroom. The only thing he could concentrate on now was his pillow.

Jessica watched in exasperation as her brother lurched back toward his room. Just then Mike came in from the kitchen, a soda in each hand.

"Ginger ale?" he offered brightly.

Jessica turned on him, her pent-up anger bubbling over. "How dare you corrupt my brother like that!" she snarled. "Did you see him? He could barely keep his eyes open."

"Hey," Mike said, shrugging his broad shoulders and spreading his hands wide, "no one held a gun to his head. He was the one who wanted to go out." He put the sodas down on the coffee table.

Jessica threw herself back against the couch. "Oh, sure," she said, her cheeks burning with anger. "As if he'd even have known where to go if you hadn't taken him." Her brother was the most levelheaded person she'd ever known, and Mike was just the opposite. "You're to blame and don't tell me you're not."

Mike shook his head. "I had nothing to do with it."

"Don't give me that," Jessica raged. "I know all about you, Mike McAllery."

"But you don't know all about your brother," Mike snapped back. "He's a big boy now and he can do what he wants. And if that means skipping a couple of classes and staying out all night, then that's his business."

Jessica sat there seething. She knew Mike was right. But it didn't make it any easier when she needed someone's help and they weren't there to give it to her. "But I need his advice," Jessica said in a small voice.

Mike took a seat across from her and leaned back in his black leather chair. "Yeah, I heard you telling Steven about Val's job offer. I say cash out and concentrate on school."

Jessica jumped to her feet. "Like I should listen to you. You laughed when I got a job and laughed even harder when I went into business with Val."

"Whoa," Mike protested. "You have to admit

that the combination of Jessica Wakefield and work is pretty hilarious."

Jessica glared down at his mocking smile. "There's nothing funny about it," she fumed. "I worked very hard. Half our success is due to me. If Steven would just look at those numbers, I'm sure it would prove that Val and I could be a major hit and that we should definitely stay in business."

Mike let out an exaggerated yawn and stretched his long legs across the low glass coffee table. "No one is saying your business wouldn't be successful. It's just that Val has a chance to work with some top-notch designers in L.A."

Jessica tossed her hair over her shoulder. "So that's who you're thinking of," she scoffed. "I should have known. This isn't about me and what would be best for me. This is about Val and her future and getting me out of the way!"

Jessica grabbed her bag and ran for the door. She didn't have to stay there and listen to her ex-husband practically announce his love for another woman. She'd seen Mike's personalized Post-its stuck all over Val's books. She knew the only way they could have gotten there was if Val had been in Mike's apartment. And there was only one explanation for that— Mike and Val were dating.

"It's such a shame," Elizabeth said, leaning forward in her black vinyl chair at the WSVU editing room. She hesitated for a split second and then deftly shifted the position of the computer graphics on the small video screen in front of her.

"Hand me the other tape, would you, please?"

Tom Watts's strong, steady hand already had it at her elbow.

We really make a great team, Elizabeth thought. She and Tom shared the same ideals, the same goals, and the same stamina when it came to going after a story. The only hard part was staying out of each other's arms when they had work to do. With Tom's piercing dark eyes and intelligent, sensuous features, that was practically a full-time job.

"What's a shame, Liz? This piece on Kitty's Restaurant came out great."

Elizabeth turned and smiled at the concerned frown on his handsome face. "Oh, not the story, Tom." The discrimination exposé on the restaurant's bra-size policy had already run. They were just doing some cleanup edits before it was stored in the station's archives. Elizabeth giggled at the thought of Tom's face when he'd seen her in the double-D padded bra she'd had to wear to work at Kitty's.

As if reading her mind Tom shook his head, wiping imaginary sweat from his forehead. "That was some getup."

"Tom," she scolded, punching his arm playfully. "Remember how much trouble you got in last time."

Even Tom had been guilty of staring at girls with large chests and using the old that's-how-guys-are excuse.

"I know, I know." He laughed. "I am not a sexist pig. I am not a sexist pig."

Elizabeth jumped into Tom's lap. "You're anything

but," she said, hugging him tight. "You're the most sensitive, sweet . . ."

"Handsome," Tom added.

"Handsome," Elizabeth agreed.

"Smart," Tom said.

"Brilliant," Elizabeth corrected him.

Tom smiled. "And lucky."

"Lucky?" Elizabeth asked.

"To have a girlfriend like you," he answered.

Elizabeth sighed, looking deep into his tender eyes. "I wish everyone could be as lucky as we are."

Tom nodded, his fingers gently tracing the curve of her cheek. "For everyone to be this lucky there would have to be a million Elizabeth Wakefields running around."

Elizabeth laughed and kissed the tip of his finger. "Elizabeths, maybe, but I don't think the Wakefield part would help too much. Look at Steven and Jessica."

"How is Steven?" Tom asked, frowning. "Have he and Billie worked things out yet?"

Elizabeth shook her head and slipped back into her own chair. "They're not even talking. That's what I meant by 'it's such a shame.'"

"Oh." Tom nodded knowingly. He reached for the completed videotape. "I was wondering when you were going to get back to that cryptic statement." He scribbled *Kitty's Restaurant, Part One* on the tape's cover and stood to shelve it in the archives.

Elizabeth smiled wryly. "And here I thought you could read my mind."

Tom turned and grinned at her. "You know

19

that's not true." He dropped down in the desk chair next to her and squeezed her hand. "But at least we agree on the important stuff."

Elizabeth smiled mischievously. "Like wanting a small wedding."

"And not wanting to get married yet." Tom laughed. "Too bad everyone's broken engagement couldn't end up as nicely as ours."

"That's for sure," Elizabeth said. For a moment her eyes clouded.

Their "engagement" had started out as a joke. During all of Billie and Steven's wedding madness, she and Tom had fought almost as much as the bride- and bridegroom-to-be. They'd finally agreed on one thing and that was the kind of wedding each of them would want. Small, private, and quiet. Not the bedlam that Billie and Steven were planning. Tom had joked that after all their fighting, he and Elizabeth shouldn't let the moment of harmony pass and he'd "proposed." She'd laughed too and "accepted."

But the longer the joke went on, the less sure she was that Tom was only kidding. Thankfully, it had turned out that he felt the same way. He was afraid that *she* had been the serious one. Neither of them was ready to get married anytime soon. But Tom was holding on to the engagement ring they'd picked out for the day when they were ready.

Elizabeth pushed a stray wisp of golden blond hair from her face. "I wish there was something I could do for Steven and Billie. Jess and I were over at Billie's this morning. She's putting up a brave front, but she's not doing well at all. She looks terrible. Wiped out. It's obvious how much she misses Steven."

Tom shifted in his seat. "What about Steven?"

Elizabeth shrugged, suddenly feeling very sad. "I don't know. I haven't spoken to him. But Billie said she saw him coming home with Mike this morning. They'd been out all night. And Steven skipped his morning class." Her eyes darkened for a second. "That can't be good."

Tom leaned toward her so she could rest her head against his shoulder. "Don't worry," he murmured, wrapping his arms around her. "Your brother just needs to blow off some steam. From what you've told me, Steven's always been incredibly responsible. Especially during Billie's pregnancy and everything." Tom brushed his lips against Elizabeth's forehead. "He probably needs to be irresponsible for a little while. He'll come to his senses."

"I hope so," Elizabeth mumbled into Tom's shoulder. She'd hate it if Steven turned into another Mike McAllery. She loved her big brother just the way he was.

Chapter Two

"I'm here to see Mr. Fowler, please," Lila said to the man at the front desk of the Downtowner Hotel. The hotel's lobby was plush, its burgundy carpeting so thick Lila felt as if she were walking on clouds.

The concierge looked slightly confused. "You're free to go right up, Ms. Fowler. I remember you."

"I'd prefer to be announced," Lila said. The man seemed to stand a little straighter as he took in her banker-blue pin-striped suit, red scarf, and brown leather briefcase. "I have an appointment," she added, smiling.

She'd torn her closet apart putting her outfit together. *No more Daddy's little girl for me,* she thought. She was tired of being treated like sugar and spice with nothing but fluff filling her brain. It was high time she was taken seriously.

The concierge picked up his phone and dialed a number. "Mr. Fowler," he said, "there is a Ms. Fowler here to see you."

"Thank you," Lila said, and strode toward the elevators. Her father always stayed in the same suite of rooms when he had business overnight in downtown Sweet Valley. But going up unannounced wouldn't have been very businesslike. *And this is definitely not a social call,* she thought.

"Lila," her father greeted her at the door, his arms outstretched. As usual her father was dressed in a crisp blue business suit, starched white shirt, and colorful tie. A carefully folded handkerchief peeked out of the breast pocket of his jacket.

"Hello, Father," Lila said, holding out her hand. Her long nails shimmered with a hint of clear polish—feminine, but not overpowering.

He raised one eyebrow and took her hand. "I guess you really mean business."

"Yes," Lila said, shaking his hand firmly. Her father had always said he could read a business opponent by the strength of his handshake. She wanted to let him know right from the start that she was no pushover.

Mr. Fowler ushered her into the imposing suite of rooms. A computer sat on the sprawling mahogany desk near the door, displaying a sophisticated spreadsheet of figures. On the small table beside the desk a newly printed page fell into the overflowing tray of a fax machine.

Mr. Fowler closed the door and walked over to the minibar. "The usual?" he asked, pouring her a Perrier. "Perhaps you'd like a cigar to go with it?" He laughed.

Lila felt the blood rise to her face. "I was going to let you off easy. But I guess you'll have to learn the hard way."

24

"Okay, joke's over," Mr. Fowler said, handing her the drink. "What's this all about? Penny told me you called, but she couldn't tell me why. Since when do you call my secretary to make an appointment? Is this about a raise in your allowance?"

Lila took a seat at the large conference table that occupied the middle of the room and snapped open her briefcase. She extracted a file folder, a yellow legal pad, two ballpoint pens, and a calculator. This was going to be fun.

"I met a man who works for you this afternoon," she said. "A man named Mr. Petty."

"Yes?" her father said, taking a seat across from her. "He's doing some legwork on one of our projects."

"So I gather," Lila said, swirling the ice around in her drink. "Seems he was interested in finding out who owns a small doughnut shop on Tyler Street and Grove."

"That's right," Mr. Fowler agreed. "I'm looking to purchase that property."

"Is it an important piece of property?" Lila asked.

"Honey," Mr. Fowler said. "Why are we wasting our time talking about business? It couldn't possibly be of any interest to you."

"That's where you're wrong," Lila said forcefully. She opened the file folder and passed the property deed inside it across the table. "If you examine this, you'll see that piece of property happens to be mine."

Her father's stunned expression was more than she had hoped for. He scanned the deed, pushing back the distinguished gray hair at his temples. She certainly had his attention now.

"And first thing tomorrow morning," she went on, "I'm going to sign this deed over to a charitable organization. Unless, that is, you can make it worth my while not to."

Mr. Fowler leapt to his feet. "You'll do no such thing, Lila. I need that property. My whole project rests on that extra square footage."

"Father," Lila said in mock surprise, "you're slipping up. Didn't you always say never let your opponent see how much you need what he has?"

Mr. Fowler growled, "What do you want?"

"Give me a figure," Lila said. "And then I'll double it. Isn't that what you always do?"

Her father grinned. "And I thought you never listened." He walked over to the minibar and poured himself a Perrier.

"I was listening, all right," Lila called after him. "And don't try to charm me. Until the contract is signed, I'm staying on my guard."

Mr. Fowler took a sip of his drink. "If I have to pay more for that property than I wanted, it will have to come out of your allowance."

Lila shrugged. "Then we'll have to write a proviso into the contract protecting my allowance as well."

Mr. Fowler grimaced and turned away. But not before Lila noticed a small smile on his lips and a grudging admiration in his eyes. "You're going to make one tough negotiator."

Lila smiled and clicked on her pen. "Why don't you have a seat and we'll find out exactly how tough."

*   *   *

Mike chalked up the end of his pool cue, looking skeptically at Steven's latest feeble attempt at a shot. They'd been at the table in the back room of the Last Stop Bar for less than ten seconds when it became obvious that Steven didn't know one end of a pool cue from the other.

"No," Mike said, taking a step forward and blocking Steven's shot. If he'd let him shoot like that, Steven would have ripped the table's felt. And while Mike was one of the Last Stop's best customers, they wouldn't take it too kindly if he let one of his amateur friends wreck the place.

"I'll never get the hang of this," Steven complained.

"Sure you will," Mike said. "Let me show you. It's all in the bridge." Mike showed Steven the easiest way he knew to hold the cue, resting the tip on his third finger. "After all, I taught your sister. I should be able to teach you."

"You brought Jess here?" Steven asked, his mouth dropping.

Mike made a face. "Of course not. This is a guys' place. Girls like your sister don't come in here." He didn't bother to tell Steven how Jessica had once followed him in and thrown a fit when she saw him with a curvy brunette.

"I'm going to get another beer," Steven said, motioning to the bar. "Are you ready?"

"Always," Mike said, downing his drink. He wasn't the kind to turn down another round. With Steven taking care of business, Mike bent over the pool table and smoothly knocked in the rest of the balls.

Steven came back with two frosted mugs of beer.

Mike took a big gulp of his. "Nothing like an ice-cold brew," he said. "Here's to bachelorhood."

"Amen," Steven said, taking a sip. "I like your thinking."

Mike grinned. It was good to be appreciated.

"And I like this place," Steven added.

"Yeah," Mike agreed, looking around. The Last Stop Bar was one of his favorite hangouts. Photos of former boxing legends hung on the dingy gray walls. The floor was covered with age-old sawdust and the tired leather seats were ripped in places. But it had a good feel to it. "This place has no airs, no pretensions," Mike said. "It's a place where a man can be a man."

Two sexy women in low-cut tops and tight jeans walked by almost in time to the slow, smoky-sounding blues that filtered into the back room from the main bar area. One of the women winked at them.

Mike winked back and then laughed as he watched Steven's eyes widen into dazed circles. "You've been cooped up too long, my man. It's time to introduce you to the real world."

"That's why I'm here," Steven said, and gulped down the rest of his beer. "My whole life I've been Mr. Responsibility. Now it's time I started having some fun."

"Well," Mike said, "you've come to the right guy to show you how to do that."

A fiery redhead Mike had occasionally dated walked by and threw her arms around him, planting a big wet kiss on his cheek. "Mike," she cooed, "c'mon and buy me a drink."

"Whoa," he said, extracting her from around his neck. "Be a good girl now—I've got to take a rain check."

Steven shook his head in wonderment.

"Hey." Mike shrugged. "Natural sex appeal."

"You've got it made," Steven said. "Beautiful babes. No responsibility. Not caring about anyone but yourself. That's the life for me."

Mike found himself grinning and nodding to each thing Steven said until he got to the "not caring about anyone" part. Then he felt as if he'd been punched in the gut. Was that what he was about? Not caring about anyone but himself?

Mike scowled. "Thanks a lot, pal. It's nice to know my closest friends consider me a selfish creep." *But isn't that exactly what I am?* he silently asked himself.

Steven gave him a sour look. "You know what I mean. And I wouldn't complain if I were you. You can have a different woman every night." Steven shrugged. "What's so bad about that? If that were my life, I wouldn't have to get all torn up inside about just one."

"Maybe," Mike mumbled, turning away to order another round. Sure, he could get a different woman every night, but when he stopped and was honest with himself, he had to admit he still got torn up by one very special woman.

"Whoops," he heard Steven say.

He turned around. *Make that one very special woman whose brother has just torn the felt on the Last Stop's pool table.*

*   *   *

29

Bruce watched Lila's beautiful brown eyes flicker in the glow of the candlelight. To celebrate their making up, he was treating her to dinner at the best restaurant in town. Not Louie's, where the other SVU students went on big dates, but to La Cage Imaginaire, a small, exclusive bistro. He hoped Lila was suitably impressed. The meal was costing him a bundle. Not that anything was too good for Lila.

"How do you like the restaurant?" Bruce asked, in case she hadn't noticed. "Isn't the food great?" He looked over at her plate. Lila had hardly touched her prosciutto and melon appetizer, while he'd already finished his garlic shrimp platter. "Aren't you hungry?"

"Bruce," Lila said, her bottom lip pouting. "I was just getting to the good part of my story."

"Sorry." Bruce extracted the ice-cold bottle from the silver champagne bucket beside the table and poured more exotic sparkling water into each of their wineglasses. For the past ten minutes Lila had been telling him about her meeting with her father. Frankly he wished she'd turn her attention to him.

"So then Daddy tried to act like the property wasn't important," Lila said.

Bruce reached out and tucked a strand of her glossy chestnut hair behind her ear. "But we knew it was."

"Of course." Lila pushed away his hand impatiently. "Why would he send his top henchman if it wasn't important? But I didn't let him know I knew that yet."

"No," Bruce said, pressing his knee against hers underneath the table. "You played it cool."

"Exactly." Lila shifted in her seat so they were no longer touching. "I let him make the first move and then I told him I owned Lila's Doughnuts."

"He must have been shocked," Bruce murmured. *I know I would have been.*

"Shocked," Lila said triumphantly, "and too far gone in the deal. He had no choice but to pay my price."

Bruce laughed and grabbed her hand. "Good work." Now maybe he'd get some attention.

Lila leaned forward, a satisfied look on her face. "Bruce, I got *three times* the price he'd wanted to pay. Plus five percent of Fowler Enterprises' profits from the project will go to the Sweet Valley Coalition for Battered Women. And the coalition gets one floor rent-free, to use as office space."

"Wow," Bruce gasped. "You got all that?"

Lila's eyes lit up with a predatory gleam. "Once you've got them on the run, you go in for the kill."

Bruce's eyebrows shot up. "But he's your father."

Lila's lips twitched. "All's fair in love and business," she said flippantly, her eyes positively glowing.

Bruce felt a cold shiver go up his spine. Was this woman safe to be with? If she would take advantage of her own father—the man who'd brought her into the world and taken care of her for the first eighteen years of her life—what would she do to a husband? He shuddered at the thought.

Bruce looked at Lila, and to his horror her features began to change. In her beautiful soft brown eyes he saw dollar signs, and her straight, even white teeth were turning into fangs. He tore his eyes away and to his fright saw his own distorted reflection in his glass. A bag man living in an abandoned car, stuffing his tattered clothes with newspapers to keep warm. And there was Lila, now the former Mrs. Bruce Patman, driving past him in a big Rolls-Royce, its vanity plate advertising the source of her wealth: WAS HIS.

It must be the garlic, he thought. His mother was allergic to garlic. She had nightmares every time she ate it. But this was no dream. He was wide awake.

"Lila," Bruce said, shaking off the thought, "sweetheart."

"Yes?" Lila said innocently, the power-mad face he'd seen in his fantasy disappearing.

"I was thinking . . . with all this talk about contracts and deals, maybe we should have one between us."

Lila frowned. "What do you mean?"

"Well." Bruce hesitated, trying to find the right words. "You know I'm crazy about you, and I think you're pretty crazy about me."

Lila nodded. "That's right." She took a sip of her water.

"Well," Bruce stumbled on. "I thought that since most modern couples have prenuptial agreements, and we're a modern couple . . ."

He looked over at Lila, but she wasn't saying anything. Had he insulted her?

"I mean," he went on hastily, "I know we're nowhere near the engagement phase yet, but when we are, and I hope we will be, I know my trustee will insist on a prenuptial agreement." He stopped and waited for the blast.

Lila sat straighter in her chair. "Great idea."

"Is it?" Bruce asked, alarmed. If Lila thought it was such a great idea, maybe he was missing something. He'd expected at least a hesitation or some type of resistance.

"Sure," Lila agreed. "It would be good practice for our business negotiation skills."

"Oh," Bruce said, letting out a small stream of air. Right. "Maybe for fun we could start roughing out an agreement now? To see where it takes us."

Lila smiled. "Fine with me."

"We'll call it a pre-engagement prenuptial agreement," Bruce said happily. *But wait a minute,* he thought. The tingling in his spine had started up again. Was it the candlelight or did he detect that predatory twinkle back in Lila's eyes?

"This is great," Steven said, as much to himself as the stranger sitting next to him at the bar. Mike was off somewhere in the other room, shooting pool. Steven had just bought the bar a round of drinks.

"That's for s-s-sure," the guy next to him slurred. Pale neon from one of the signs behind the bar bathed his face in a sickly green light. "Absolutely."

Steven drummed his fingers on the bar. "I mean, I can stay out as late as I want. I don't have to let anyone know where I am or what I'm doing. I can have fun like this every night."

33

"Yep," the guy next to him agreed. His head gave several exaggerated shakes.

Steven swiveled on his bar stool. "There are a million beautiful girls out there waiting to meet me. And now that I'm single, I can meet them all."

The guy made a noise.

Steven wasn't sure if it was another "Yep" or a burp, but he went on. "Girls who would appreciate me," he said. "Who would love to have me as their husband. Not that I'm going to get married now. Not me, not ever. I'm going to hang out in bars like this every night, me and the guys."

The man gave a slight nod and then dropped his head in his arms.

"What do I need with all that domestic stuff?" Steven continued. "That was a big weight around my neck. This is so much more fun." He stopped and took a sip of his beer. Even he could hear the phony enthusiasm in his voice. Who was he trying to kid? This wasn't fun. This was a major drag. He missed Billie. If they were still together, they'd be snuggled up in front of the TV right now, munching popcorn. Their favorite show was on tonight. *Is she watching it without me?*

"Do you always talk to yourself?" a sexy voice murmured.

Steven turned and looked straight into the eyes of a beautiful, blue-eyed blond. She wore a tight, hot-pink cotton top that accented her bloodred lipstick and painted nails. Steven felt his mouth drop open as the woman smiled at him, her long, straw-colored hair tumbling seductively over her right eye.

"I was talking to him," Steven managed, throwing back his shoulders. He motioned to the guy next to him, who, as if on cue, began to snore.

The girl gave him an amused look. "Doesn't seem like much of a companion." She eased herself onto the battered leather stool next to Steven's, like hot fudge pouring over a sundae. He wondered if the seat would begin to melt like a scoop of vanilla ice cream.

"No, I guess not," Steven agreed.

"Do you come here a lot?" the girl asked. She pulled a pack of cigarettes and a lighter out of her slim black handbag, tapping one cigarette free.

This is easier than I thought, Steven said to himself, frowning. *But wasn't that supposed to be my line?*

"Not a lot," Steven said.

The girl tossed back her hair and laughed. "You're putting me on. I'm sure I saw you here last week." The unlit cigarette dangled from the corner of her mouth.

Steven shrugged. *Last week I was still with Billie,* he thought. He hadn't even known that this place existed. "I could have been here for a little while." He smiled.

The girl lit her cigarette, the flame from her lighter dancing in her eyes. "I knew it. I never forget a face."

"That's lucky for me, then," Steven said.

The girl laughed again, exhaling a cloud of smoke. "I think it's safe to say you're having a very lucky night. Listen, I don't live far from here," she purred, leaning toward him. Suddenly Steven found himself looking deep into her blue eyes. "In fact," she whispered, drawing so close that Steven could feel her breath on his neck, "I'm right around the corner. I thought I might make it an early night. Why don't you come along?"

Steven gulped. He was single and free, and a beautiful woman had materialized out of nowhere and just invited him home. This was everything he wanted, right?

Steven hesitated for a split second and then scooped up his change. "Sure," he said, getting to his feet. "I'll come along."

The girl wrapped her arm around his and led him out to the street. As the music from the Last Stop faded away, Steven became aware of the occasional scrape of her high heels against the pavement. He could smell the stale smoke and sawdust of the bar in the girl's hair. Under the streetlights her long red nails seemed to flash at him like the cruel talons of some bird of prey. He stopped when they reached the corner. He could feel her pulling on him, but he held steady.

"I turn left here," Steven said firmly, extracting himself from her grip. The girl stared up at him in angry amazement. "That's my way home." *After all*, he thought, *I don't even know your name.*

"Who could that be at this hour?" Billie asked herself, slipping into a pair of jeans and pulling an old sweatshirt over the T-shirt she slept in. It *was* only ten o'clock at night, but she'd been ready for bed, her face scrubbed clean and her hair brushed out, for the past hour. With Steven gone, she found the easiest way to pass the time was by sleeping.

But maybe that's Steven now. She ran to her front door and peered through the peephole. The lean, good-looking face of Chas Brezinski, her friend from the music department, smiled back. Chas's long, sandy brown hair was tucked casually behind his ears and lay loose against his broad shoulders. His white cotton shirt was unbuttoned at the collar, displaying a leather necklace with a colorfully painted pottery bead at its center.

Billie paused, her hand on the doorknob. She'd been ready to fling open the door if Steven had been there. But now looking down at her rumpled clothes, she felt uncomfortable. She wasn't exactly dressed for visitors. Oh, well. Chas was a close friend—he wouldn't mind.

As she opened the door, Chas produced a beautiful bouquet of delicate purple and blue flowers from behind his back. "Don't ask me what they are." He laughed, his blue eyes twinkling. "I told the florist I needed something happy to cheer up a friend."

Billie smiled wanly. "They're beautiful, Chas. Thanks." She motioned him in. "Take a seat. I'll get a vase."

Billie walked slowly through to the kitchen. "I really am glad Chas came over," she told herself. He was a great guy and a good friend.

"But he's not Steven," a small voice inside her answered back.

Billie shook her head and reminded herself that it was Chas who'd given her the courage and confidence to pursue her guitar studies and try out for the scholarship to Spain. He was understanding and supportive about her music, unlike Steven. Billie bit her lip. "Stop thinking about Steven," she whispered to herself.

"Can I help?" Chas called out.

"I'm going to make some herbal tea," Billie called back. "Would you like milk and honey in yours?"

"Sure," Chas said, coming up behind her. "Just a bit of honey, please." He sat at the kitchen table, taking the chair nearest the refrigerator.

Billie filled the teakettle with water and placed it on the stove. She frowned to herself. Something wasn't right. Why did she feel so strange with Chas sitting there? Was it because he was in Steven's seat? Or was it the way Chas's eyes seemed to follow her every move? She looked over at him, wondering if she was imagining things. But when she caught his gaze, his full lips smiled back at her in a way they had never done before.

"What is it?" she asked, her voice strained.

"Those flowers." Chas continued to smile at her. "They make your eyes look almost purple. A beautiful purple."

Billie felt herself blush and turned away. She reached into the cupboard for two mugs. "Could you get out the milk?" she mumbled.

He leaned back in his chair and opened the refrigerator. "Billie," he said, his voice sounding tentative. "I know this probably isn't the best time." He placed the milk carton on the kitchen table.

Billie held her breath. Chas was going to ask her out. She knew it. That was what the flowers and the strange look on his face were about. And why not? She and Chas seemed like a perfect match. They both loved music. They didn't see it as a hobby, like Steven did, but instead as a dream to be pursued. Chas was kind and understanding. Not at all overbearing and headstrong like Steven. *And let's face it,* Billie thought, *Chas is a total hunk, too.* What could be more perfect? Still, she had never thought of Chas in romantic terms, despite what Steven might have thought.

"I was wondering if you and I . . ." He faltered.

Billie knew she should interject now if she wanted to go out with Chas. Make it easier for him. Give him some encouragement. But her mouth wouldn't open.

He started toying with the milk carton. "What I mean is," he stumbled. "Well, would you consider going out with me?"

Billie hesitated and then took a seat at the table across from him. "Chas, I . . . um," she stammered. Their common love of music and Chas's sensitivity were great reasons to go out with him. But it was her heart that made the final decision. "I . . . can't, Chas." She shook her head sadly. She didn't want to hurt him.

Billie reached for his hand and squeezed it. "Even though Steven and I have broken up, I'm still in love with him." It felt good to say it to someone, even though she knew it wasn't what Chas wanted to hear.

Chas hung his head. "I was afraid of that." He pulled his hand away. "I hope we'll still be friends, though."

"Of course," Billie said, smiling.

Chas stood up. "I should go."

Billie walked him downstairs. Chas's sporty little pickup truck was parked right outside her apartment building.

"If you change your mind—," Chas began, getting into the bright blue truck.

"I'll know exactly who to call," Billie finished, leaning over and giving him a quick peck on the cheek.

She straightened up to find Steven standing in the street a few yards away. He stared at her, his eyes blazing an angry red.

"Steven," she said, shock waves running through her body. "Chas and I were just—"

"Kissing," he snapped. "And it's none of my business." He stormed off, letting the front door of the apartment building slam shut.

"I'm sorry." Chas started to reopen his door. "I'll talk to him if you want."

"No," Billie said, feeling her own anger rising. "If Steven wants to know the truth, he can come and talk to me."

Steven bounded up the stairs two at a time. He was so blinded by rage he didn't even see Tom coming the other way until he banged into him just outside Mike's apartment. "What are you doing here?" Steven snapped.

Tom put up his hands. "Hey, I was just picking up some chem notes from George Blake down the hall. What's the matter?"

Steven slammed his fist against the wall. "Ow,"

he yelled, hugging his bruised knuckles to his chest. "Damn that Chas," he shouted. "I should have pulled him out of that truck and taught him a lesson."

"Calm down. What happened?"

Steven unlocked the door and stomped into Mike's apartment, kicking at the furniture and cursing under his breath. Tom followed him inside. "He moved in on Billie the minute my back was turned. I knew it. I said it all along. That creep's had a thing for her since she started playing guitar."

"Sit," Tom demanded. "Tell me what you're talking about."

Steven threw himself down on the dark leather couch. "I'm talking about Billie and Chas. I was just coming in and I found Mr. Music Lover kissing Billie in the parking lot."

"Are you sure?" Tom asked.

Steven pointed to his eyes. "I saw it." He clenched his fists. "Chas was in his car, and Billie was bent over kissing him through the window."

Tom sighed. "She was probably giving him a good-night peck. They are friends, after all."

"At this hour?" Steven growled. "Who knows how long they'd been at it before I showed up. I bet he was up in the apartment with her, too. *My* apartment!"

Tom sat down on the leather chair across from him. "I wouldn't jump to conclusions, Steven. Liz was with Billie this morning and told me Billie was really broken up about your moving out."

"Well, she's repaired now," Steven scoffed.

Tom shook his head. "You don't know what's

going on. Why don't you go up there and talk to her?"

Steven flexed his hand. It was throbbing from the punch he'd given the wall. "It's no use," he mumbled. "Every time I try and talk to Billie, we end up shouting at each other." Steven turned his face away. *And since the miscarriage,* he thought, *the only thing we've said to each other was that the wedding's off and I should move out.*

Tom got up. "You've got to talk to her. It's the only way you'll work this out." Steven felt Tom's hand on his shoulder. "Look, I've got to go. Your sister's waiting for me in the library."

Steven turned to look at him. "She's got you on a short leash, my man," he spat out.

Tom's mouth dropped open and Steven winced.

"I'm sorry, Tom. I don't know why I said that. This thing with Billie has gotten me all messed up."

Tom straightened, his jaw tight and his eyes narrowed. "No, maybe you meant what you said and *that's* what your problem really is all about."

Steven sat up. "What are you saying?"

Tom started for the door. "Think about it."

"No, come on," Steven called, jumping to his feet. "What are you trying to say?"

Tom twirled around, pointing his finger at Steven. "Get this straight. I'm going to meet Liz because I *want* to, not because anyone is twisting my arm."

Steven frowned. "And I want to be with Billie for the same reason." He shrugged. "Why do you think I was prepared to marry her? I was ready to take care of her, to graduate early and get a job."

Tom threw up his hands. "Prepared? Steven, listen to the words you're using. Where are love and desire? All I hear is talk about responsibility."

"What's wrong with—" Steven stopped. *Wait a minute,* he thought, a light exploding in his brain. *All I ever did was let Billie know I would do my duty. Like a wooden soldier about to die in battle. There was no romance in that. Did Chas offer to be her new boyfriend by saying it was his duty? No way.*

Steven smiled for what felt like the first time in days. It was all so simple. He wanted to be with Billie because he loved her, not because it was his obligation. He'd been so busy trying to make the right decisions that he'd forgotten to tell her how he felt about her. He didn't want to break up. And if it wasn't too late, maybe she would take him back.

Chapter Three

Mike looked up from the Last Stop's pool table as Steven ran into the room. It was nearly midnight. "Hey, buddy," Mike said. "I thought you went home."

Steven was out of breath. He stood there gasping for a second. "Not quite," he said, "but with a little luck and your help I might actually get home tonight." He came around the table, practically pulling the cue out of Mike's hands. "C'mon," he said, "we've got to go."

"Hold on." Mike shook his head. "You're going too fast for me." He was a couple of balls away from clearing the whole table. And there was ten bucks riding on the outcome.

"Sorry," Steven said, grinning. "I've realized how stupid I've been. Look, I want to get back with Billie."

"I could have told you that," Mike said, reaching for his beer with his free hand. All Steven's talk about loving the freedom of single life hadn't fooled Mike. Anyone could see that the guy was still crazy about Billie.

"But if I want to get her back, I have to show her how I feel. You know . . . romance her."

Mike laughed. "I could have told you that, too. That's what every woman needs." He tilted back his glass and finished his beer.

Steven started to pace. "I want to serenade her, but I need a horn to do it."

Mike put his empty mug back on the table. "Can you even play a horn?" Nothing was less romantic than a pair of shattered eardrums.

Steven shrugged. "Sort of, but it's the thought that counts."

Joey, Mike's opponent, leaned in between them. "Hey, we gonna be here all night?"

"Chill out a second," Mike said as he began lining up his next shot. He would pocket the six ball and then the eight. That is, if he could avoid having the cue ball settle in Steven's now infamous tear in the felt.

"Hey," Steven said, this time actually pulling the cue out of Mike's hands. "Are you listening? I need to get a horn. Now."

"At this hour?" Mike said. "Forget about it. Nothing's open."

"It's got to be tonight," Steven said. "I'm going to lose her if I don't do something. I can feel it in my bones."

"Okay, okay." Mike relented. He tossed a ten-dollar bill onto the table, to Joey's astonishment. *Next time you won't be so lucky, pal*, he thought.

46

Mike turned to Steven. "I know one place, maybe." At that hour all the respectable pawn shops were closed. But Mama Rosa might have a horn at her place. The problem was Mama ground guys like Steven up for breakfast. "If you keep your mouth shut and let me do all the talking, it might work."

Mama's shop was operated out of a small storefront down the street from the Last Stop Bar. From the outside the place looked deserted. The neon sign was off and the shades were drawn.

Mike rapped firmly on the door and then stepped back. Mama was farsighted and didn't like it when her customers stood too close to the peephole.

"Who is it?" a gravelly voice called out.

"Mac," Mike said, "and my friend, Heartbreak."

"Heartbreak?" Steven asked, frowning.

Mike grinned. "Nobody uses their real name when they come to see Mama. Heartbreak sounds better than Lovesick."

The door creaked open a fraction of an inch, throwing a small wedge of light onto the pavement outside. The gravelly voice said, "What do you want?"

"We're looking for a horn, Mama," Mike said. *A little white lie might help,* he thought. "My friend here plays in a band and they've got a big audition tonight."

"What's it to me?"

"How much you got?" Mike whispered, elbowing Steven.

Steven reached into his pocket. "Thirty dollars."

"Leave it there," Mike ordered. "Twenty bucks, Mama—it's for a good cause."

"Not interested," the gravelly voice spit back.

"Thirty, then," Mike said, "but not a penny more."

"Humph," Mama said. "What do I care whether some guy plays for some band or not?"

"You got a point there, Mama, but thirty bucks is thirty bucks," Mike said. "And I guess I could throw in an extra ten."

Mama made a noise that sounded like a cross between a lion and a steam engine. But Mike felt sure she was coming around. Ten more bucks and he knew he'd have her.

Then suddenly Steven gave him a shove.

"Hey," Mike said, trying to get his balance. "What's the big idea?" Steven was going to blow everything!

Steven ignored him and stepped into the crack of light. "It's not for a band," he admitted. "It's to serenade my girlfriend. I'm going to lose her if I don't do something to show her how much I love her."

Oh no, Mike thought, grimacing. *He's ruined it.* Not only would they never get a horn now, he'd never be able to show his face in Mama Rosa's again. He'd kill Steven for this.

But to his amazement the door swung wide open on its creaking hinges. Mama Rosa stood there, her hard face softened by a smile.

"Why didn't you say so, Mac?" she said. "The horns are in the back, Heartbreak. Take any one of them. On the house."

Mike grinned as Steven hurried into the shop. Maybe love and tough guys wasn't such a bad combination after all.

*   *   *

Billie leapt out of bed. "What is that horrible noise?" she shouted. It was worse than someone scraping their nails on a blackboard. She grabbed her robe and ran to the window. Should she call the police? Surely someone needed help. *And if not, then they should be arrested for disturbing the peace,* she thought.

She craned her neck, trying to make out the dark figure in the shadows of the parking lot. As the figure stepped out into the moonlight, she realized that it was a battered French horn causing that racket.

"That's *Steven*!" she said to herself, her heart leaping. And he was playing the tune to their favorite TV show. The show that tonight, for the first time she could remember, she'd watched alone.

She flung open her bedroom window. "What are you doing?" she called. "You'll wake up the neighbors."

Steven took the horn from his lips. "I don't care. I want everyone to know. I'll shout it from the rooftops."

"What?" Billie asked, her bottom lip beginning to tremble.

"I love Billie Winkler," Steven declared.

"What?" Billie whispered. Did he really mean it?

Steven threw open his arms. "I love you," he shouted.

Lights had started turning on throughout the building. People were poking their heads out windows to watch.

Billie leaned farther out the window, her eyes

filling with tears as she stared down at Steven's handsome, earnest face. "Are you sure?"

"I've never been more sure of anything in my life," Steven shouted. "I love Billie Winkler and I want the whole world to know it!"

"The whole world does know it, kid," a man's tired voice yelled. "Now keep it down. Some of us are trying to sleep."

"You keep it down, Mr. Grumpy," a woman's voice called back. "Let the lovebirds speak."

"Go on, young man," another voice said. "This sure beats the late movie."

"Billie," Steven said, "I'm sorry for acting like such a coldhearted loser. I vow from now on to be the most romantic, loving, sensitive guy in the world. If you give me another chance, I'll never let you down again."

Billie felt her heart swell, the tension and sadness of the past weeks melting away.

"Listen to him, young lady," the grumpy man shouted. "He must mean it. He's gotten us all out of bed."

"Can I come up?" Steven asked.

Billie hesitated, looking at Steven, at the horn, at all the expectant faces in the lighted windows. "Of course," she shouted. "I love you too."

As Steven ran for the front door the complex erupted in applause.

Billie waited for him in the hallway and hugged him with all her might. There were tears in her eyes.

"I love you," Steven murmured, running his strong hands through her hair. "I'm so sorry."

Billie led him into their apartment. "I'm sorry

too." She buried her face against his chest. "I never meant for you to move out." It felt like heaven to be held in his arms again.

Steven lifted her face toward his and brushed away her tears. "I shouldn't have left."

"Let's never break up again." Billie sighed, meaning it from the bottom of her heart.

"Don't worry, we won't." Steven dropped down on one knee. "Billie Winkler, will you marry me?"

"Ten black, eight brown, two dozen green," Jessica said, quickly counting off spools of thread. It was early morning. She and Val Tripler were taking inventory in a far corner of the airy loft they'd rented for their fashion business.

Jessica stepped down from the short ladder she'd been standing on. They still had rows and rows of green industrial shelving to check.

Val made a note on her clipboard and pushed a lock of her shoulder-length auburn hair behind her ear. Corkscrew earrings, a black turtleneck, matching slacks, and a pair of clunky Doc Martens announced Val's creative streak to the world.

"Any red, Jess?" Val asked.

"Nope, no red." Jessica sighed inwardly. When Val had said they needed to take "inventory," Jessica had thought Val wanted to have a heart-to-heart about the future of their business. But as usual, Val had meant exactly what she'd said.

"And there's no white, either," Jessica added.

Val nodded. "Used it all on the blouses." She made another note on her clipboard.

Time for a break, Jessica thought, pushing herself

up onto one of the long, low tables that filled the loft's spacious work area. She stretched out her slim legs. She was glad she'd worn her black leggings and a loose white painter smock. Rooting around those dusty shelves and all their leftover supplies would definitely have been uncomfortable in the tight purple skirt she'd almost worn that morning.

"Getting tired?" Val asked.

"A little," Jessica admitted. "This isn't as much fun as the fashion show." She blew a strand of golden hair from her face.

Val shrugged. "The fashion show part comes maybe four, five times a year to launch the new season. This is the day-in, day-out reality. The fashion business is all about preparation and planning." Val smiled wanly. "A little like going to class all semester before the big test."

Jessica winced. Her studies had fallen way off since she and Val had gone into business together. She'd been putting off doing anything about it until the fate of the business was decided.

She looked around the quiet loft. It was hard to imagine that less than a week ago this place had been buzzing. The Thetas had been running around for their fittings, and the seamstresses had been maniacally sewing the last of the skirts and blouses. Now the sewing machines were all silent. The tailor's dummies stood naked or oddly draped with discarded swatches of cloth.

The fashion show, launching Val's line of clothing, had been a resounding success. And a healthy chunk of the proceeds had gone to help the Sweet Valley Coalition for Battered Women.

But now the place felt lonely, with just a slight breeze stirring the floor-to-ceiling curtains around the tall windows.

Jessica's eyes fell on several boxes sitting toward the back of the workbench. She sighed and opened the first of them. "Six dozen packs of hooks and eyes, eight brown zippers, ten blue ones," she counted. "We'd better get some blue thread, too."

Val nodded and began writing again.

Jessica pulled another box toward her, opened it, and let out a low whistle. Staring up at her was a tangle of buttons, every one of them loose. At a glance she couldn't tell if there was a matched pair in the bunch.

"Not a pretty picture," Val said, putting down her clipboard and jumping up to join Jessica on the long workbench. "Better dump some out and we'll start matching them up."

Jessica groaned and spilled out most of the box. "Just think, when we get really famous, we can hire people to do this."

Val laughed. "Even then, this work is hands-on. This is where your inspiration comes from. Just look." She laid out five seemingly incongruous buttons in a line. "See how great they look together?"

Jessica nodded. She never would have thought to put a gold button with a silver one, let alone combine those metals with the three basic colors of red, black, and blue. But all together it really worked.

"How did you do that?" Jessica asked. "That's amazing."

53

Val shrugged. "When you've been schooled in fashion as long as I have, things like that just come to you."

Jessica pulled the buttons toward her. "I wish I had an eye like yours." She experimented with a couple of different combinations, but none looked as good as Val's had. "Maybe working together will make some of your fashion sense rub off on me."

"Maybe," Val said. "But it takes time. I went to design school, don't forget. I wouldn't have been able to come up with those tops and skirts if I hadn't first learned how material drapes and how to make a pattern."

Funny, Val had been talking about school all afternoon. Come to think of it, if Val had said the word *school* once, she'd said it a hundred times.

"What are you trying to say?" Jessica asked. Suddenly she realized that Val's little speech was leading somewhere.

Val pushed a stack of buttons to one side and looked at her levelly. "Mike told me about your conversation the other day, and I agree with him, Jessica. I think you *should* stay in school."

Jessica could barely speak for a minute. Her mind was racing. Val and Mike had been discussing *her*? How dare they? A dull, sick feeling came over her. She'd thought she and Val were a team. But obviously it was Val and Mike who'd been the team all along.

"So that's the conclusion you two came to?" Jessica seethed. "Get rid of Jessica?" She jumped down from the workbench.

Val shook her head slowly. "It's not what you

think. We were both considering what was best for you. Especially Mike."

Jessica rolled her eyes. Did Val think she'd been born yesterday?

"Look," Val went on. "In my own selfish way I'd like to keep our partnership going. But Mike thinks it's better for you to finish school."

"Do you expect me to believe that?" Jessica snapped. "Mike doesn't have my best interest at heart. He just wants me out of the way so he can go out with you."

"Now wait one second," Val said, her voice rising. "You've got this all wrong. Mike and I aren't going out."

"Right," Jessica snarled, turning away. *And I don't have an identical twin,* she thought. "Then why is Mike so interested in our business?" It surely wasn't for Jessica's sake. He'd done nothing but laugh at her since the beginning. No one could deny that.

"You better ask Mike about that," Val said coolly.

Jessica grabbed another handful of buttons and started furiously sorting them. Maybe she would ask Mike. See what he had to say for himself.

"All right, let's try it again," Lila said to Bruce, crumpling up yet another piece of paper and throwing it in the vicinity of the wastepaper basket. They were sitting around a rickety old table in the upstairs lounge of Dickenson Hall, Jessica and Elizabeth's dormitory. A stack of pads and pencils and two cans of diet root beer sat on the table between them. Not exactly posh surroundings, but at least it was neutral ground.

Lila hadn't expected drafting an agreement to be so hard. After all, it was only a pre-engagement prenuptial agreement, not the real thing.

"Tell you what," she joked, "how about whatever is mine stays mine and whatever is yours *becomes* mine."

"Very funny," Bruce said, giving her a sour look. He wadded his own piece of paper into a tight ball and sent it sailing across the room, where it landed neatly in the can.

"Touché," Lila said. "Have you thought about going pro?"

They exchanged smiles. Thank goodness. At least she knew they were still capable of being civil to each other. They'd been sitting here for over an hour without being able to agree on word one.

In fact, the problem had started even *before* they'd sat down. Bruce had wanted them to write the agreement in his room. But there was no way Lila could allow that. She knew all about home-court advantage. *Never negotiate on enemy territory,* she thought.

Bruce reached for a fresh sheet of paper. "Let's try once more. But be a little more reasonable, Lila."

Lila made a face. "Me? I've been nothing but reasonable. It's only right that if we split up, I should get your Jeep, clothing, and bank account." What would Bruce need with those things? He'd be at home nursing a broken heart. She tossed back her dark chestnut hair in a dismissive gesture.

"You're the one who's making this hard. If you don't stop refusing all my suggestions, we're going to be here all night."

Bruce threw up his hands. "But my *clothes*, Lila?"

Lila shrugged. "Donating designer menswear to charity is a great tax write-off."

Bruce fumed. "And what about me? What am I supposed to wear? In fact, what do I get from *you* if we break up?"

Lila raised one perfect eyebrow. "You'll have the distinguished honor of being able to say you once went out with me."

Bruce jumped to his feet. "That's it." He slammed his fist down on the table, making their soda cans rattle. "You're not taking this seriously at all."

"I am so," Lila said, her dark brown eyes blazing. "If you break my heart, I get everything. That's how it should be."

"Who says I'll break your heart?" Bruce shouted. "It's much more likely you'll dump me and I'll end up with nothing."

Lila snapped her pencil in two. "Exactly! You obviously did something to make me dump you, so you deserve nothing."

Bruce shook his head and sat back down. He grabbed his soda and took a long swig. "I don't know. Maybe we're going about this all wrong."

"I know what you mean," Lila said. "We've been at this for ages and all we have to show for it are three broken pencils and a can full of crumpled paper."

"Don't forget all *your* paper," Bruce said with a

smirk. "You know, the pieces on the floor?"

"Hey," Lila said brightly, "that's one point we can agree on. You're the athlete. You can have all the sporting equipment."

"It's already mine," Bruce said curtly.

"Once we're a couple it will all be *ours*," Lila said. "That's what you keep forgetting."

"Ours is one thing," Bruce said. "But you're trying to make it all yours."

"I am not!" Lila shouted. "I just said you could have the sporting equipment." Why was he being so unreasonable?

"And I just told you," Bruce said, "it's already mine."

Lila sank her head in her hands. "You're right," she mumbled, "this isn't working. Maybe *we* don't work."

"No," Bruce said, getting up and going over to her. "That's exactly my point. We do work. Just this—" He swept his hand around to indicate the pencils and the legal pads. "This doesn't work."

"So what should we do?" Lila asked miserably. It had been a lot easier negotiating with her father.

"Let's go back to being Bruce and Lila, couple in love," Bruce said.

Lila smiled. That sounded like a great idea. "And forget about the pre-engagement prenuptial agreement?"

"Sure," Bruce said. "We have our love to keep us together. We don't need a contract for that."

"Right," Lila said. After all, what was a piece of paper against the strength of their love?

Bruce reached for her. "Let's seal that with a kiss."

Lila giggled, falling against his strong, muscular chest. "We'd better make it a good one," she said, "if we want it to be binding in a court of law."

But the words were lost as his lips passionately explored hers.

Bruce pulled back from Lila's tawny limbs to catch his breath. Her perfume was intoxicating. *I need to keep my wits about me,* he thought. If there was one thing he'd learned in life, it was that it was better to stay cool under fire. And being in an embrace with Lila was definitely like being on fire.

She walked her fingers up the back of his spine, setting off small explosions in his brain. He gritted his teeth. He needed a moment to collect his thoughts. What were they talking about? Right, the pre-engagement prenuptial agreement.

Lila's soft lips brushed against his, and he felt himself falling under her spell once more. He tried to focus on a spot on the wall and not let his eyes close until he remembered the rest of it. *Call your lawyer,* flashed through his mind. Right. Just because they'd decided not to work on the agreement together didn't mean he couldn't look into it on his own. What was that guy's name? *Think, Patman, think.* It had been on the tip of his tongue until Lila snuggled her body even closer to him and blew softly into his ear.

This time he was gone for a full five minutes, but still he pulled himself back. *Daniel Loeb, attorney-at-law. That was it,* he thought. *And his telephone number?*

But then Lila's lips pressed harder against his,

turning his thoughts into pudding. Suddenly the fullness of her lips was the only thing he could think about.

Lila felt herself drowning in Bruce's powerful arms and frantically searched her mind for a life preserver. She needed to get a few thoughts straight, but kissing Bruce made it almost impossible.

With superhuman mental strength she centered herself. She knew Bruce was right. They should trust their love and put aside thoughts of a pre-engagement prenuptial agreement. *But,* she thought, shivering as Bruce ran his fingers through her silky hair, *that doesn't mean I can't spend time looking into one myself.*

He kissed the sensitive nape of her neck, and now she was not only drowning but seeing stars. Somehow she had to stay focused—this was important. She'd call a lawyer, have a chat. Bruce cupped her chin and gazed deeply into her burning eyes. *A little chat.* She sighed inwardly, starting to lose herself again. Just to clear up a few technical points. . . .

"Absolutely not," Mr. Wakefield boomed. His voice ricocheted off the creamy white walls of the Wakefields' living room. "I don't think it's a good idea at all."

Steven sighed and watched his father pace back and forth along the oriental rug, his hands jammed into the pockets of his gray cardigan sweater. *Not a good idea.* How many times had he heard that? He snaked his hand along the pale peach couch to give Billie's a squeeze. He was used to his father's pronouncements. But he was afraid Billie would be upset.

"Dear, keep your voice down," Mrs. Wakefield scolded. "Shouting isn't going to get us anywhere."

That's for sure, Steven thought, looking over at Billie. If she pushed herself any deeper into the couch, she'd be behind it.

"I'm sorry," Mr. Wakefield said. "But this has got me very upset." He sat down in his oversize green easy chair.

Steven sighed. "It's not like we want to do anything drastic."

"Getting married is drastic," Mr. Wakefield asserted. His hand swung through the air as he made his point, knocking over a bowl of peanuts in the process. He leapt to his feet again.

"Ned." Mrs. Wakefield sighed. "I just vacuumed that rug."

"Sorry, dear. But if these kids don't see that marriage is drastic business, then that shows they're not ready. And there's no reason to stand here and discuss it."

"Dad," Steven said, "can we state our case?"

"Honey, sit down," Mrs. Wakefield commanded. "At least hear them out."

Mr. Wakefield sat, and Steven's mother prompted him, "Go on, Steven, we're listening."

Steven took a deep breath and straightened his shoulders. Maybe coming in and announcing that the wedding was back on hadn't been the best approach. But he and Billie had given it a lot of serious thought. They'd spent the whole night discussing it. They had no doubts this time.

61

"Billie and I love each other," Steven began.

Mr. Wakefield made a noise to interrupt.

"Dad, please," Steven pleaded, "let me finish. We love each other and after all we've been through these past couple of weeks, we've learned what kind of commitment marriage requires."

Billie squeezed his hand.

"We want to make that commitment to each other."

Mr. Wakefield shook his head. "There's no reason to get married now. Before, when Billie was expecting a baby, you had no choice."

Steven exhaled forcefully, willing himself not to lose his temper. "Now we've had time to think about it and we've decided it's what we want." He pulled Billie closer to him on the couch and wrapped his arm around her. "It's not about rushing into a situation because our backs are against the wall. It's about choosing to do something because we want to do it."

"But why now?" Mr. Wakefield asked. "You're not even finished with school yet."

"That's true," Mrs. Wakefield said. She turned to Billie. "What about your scholarship to Spain?"

Billie sat forward on the couch. "I'm going. Only now Steven will come with me. He's going to spend a semester in Spain too."

"I'll save up over the summer to pay my tuition," Steven added. It was the perfect solution. "And Dad, you always said knowing a foreign language was a real help in business. After a semester in Spain, I'll be speaking Spanish like a native."

Billie smiled. "It will be like an extended honeymoon."

Mr. Wakefield threw up his hands in frustration. "Well, it seems as if you've got it all worked out. I'm not sure why you came to us."

"Because . . ." Steven hesitated. "We'd like your blessing. Yours and Mom's."

Mr. Wakefield bent down to pick up the peanuts he'd spilled, but not before Steven caught the barest smile on his lips. He dropped the peanuts onto a napkin and sighed. "I guess your mother and I got married pretty young."

Mrs. Wakefield nodded. "My parents weren't very happy about it. And neither were your father's, if I remember correctly," she added.

Mr. Wakefield brushed some crumbs away with his hand. "But it seems to have worked out pretty well."

"Pretty well." Mrs. Wakefield winked at Steven and Billie.

"Alice?" Mr. Wakefield asked, sounding shocked.

"*Very* well, dear." Mrs. Wakefield laughed. "Wonderfully."

Mr. Wakefield let out a deep sigh and sat a bit straighter. "You've always been a sensible and responsible young man, Steven. You've never given me cause to question your judgment. And I certainly couldn't want a sweeter young woman as my daughter-in-law." Mr. Wakefield stopped and gave a big smile. "You have my blessing."

"And mine," Mrs. Wakefield said, looking very pleased.

Steven jumped up and hugged his parents. He couldn't have asked for a better family.

Mrs. Wakefield smoothed down her dress.

"Well, with that settled, we might as well stick with the original target date. That way we won't lose any of our deposits. I'll have to call the tent man and the caterer and there's the florist. . . ."

Steven tuned out and gave Billie a big kiss.

"Now I know who you inherited your practicality from," she whispered in his ear. "Let's get out of here before she puts us to work."

Steven chuckled and wrapped his arms around his bride-to-be. "Good idea." He laughed. "Let me know when the coast is clear."

Chapter Four

Elizabeth pushed aside her notebook as the waitress placed a small plate of tacos in front of her and a heaping plate of enchiladas, refried beans, and rice in front of Tom. "Can I get you anything else?" the woman asked.

Elizabeth giggled. "I don't think so." There was already a basket piled high with tortilla chips, a large bowl of guacamole dip, and two steaming mugs of coffee on the table.

Elizabeth took a bite of her taco and smiled as Tom started to wolf down his meal. "Someone's hungry."

Tom looked up, his fork poised midway to his mouth. "I'm fortifying myself for tonight's party."

Elizabeth laughed. "If you eat all that, you'll be ready to party for a year." She reached for a tortilla chip. "But you deserve it. If it wasn't for you talking to Steven last night, the wedding wouldn't be back on and we wouldn't be throwing them a surprise engagement party."

Tom shrugged and spread some more sour cream on his enchilada. "Anyone could have done it. Steven needed someone to sound off to. He would have come to his senses sooner or later."

Elizabeth smiled and took a sip of her coffee. Tom was never one to boast. He had the dark, classic good looks of a movie star and a quick, intelligent mind to match. But he never bragged or acted superior. "That's not what Steven told me."

Tom blushed and shifted in his chair uncomfortably. "So who's invited to this party?"

"Okay, no more flattery," she teased. Tom was obviously trying to change the subject. She picked up her notebook. "I've got you and me; Jessica, of course; Danny and Isabella . . ." Danny Wyatt and Isabella Ricci were one of the happiest and most attractive couples she knew. Danny's dark African-American complexion contrasted beautifully with Isabella's porcelain skin.

"Winston and Denise . . ." Winston Egbert and Denise Waters were something of an odd couple. Winston had been the class clown back at Sweet Valley High, while Denise was one of the most beautiful and sought-after women on the SVU campus.

"Alexandra and Noah . . ." Alexandra Rollins had been Elizabeth's best friend in high school. She'd been through some tough times since coming to SVU, but now that she was going out with Noah Pearson, her life seemed back on track.

"Plus a whole bunch of Steven's friends from the Prelaw Society are coming over," Elizabeth added.

Tom scooped up some beans with his fork. "Sounds like a good crowd."

Elizabeth frowned. "I'm forgetting someone." She swept her eyes over the patrons of the coffee shop. Two tables away she spied a muscular-looking, dark-haired man taking a bite of a juicy hamburger. An expensive watch glinted on his wrist. *Bruce,* she thought. "Lila and Bruce." She added their names to the list. "But there's someone else."

Tom chewed thoughtfully. "I don't know. Have you figured out where the party is going to be?"

Elizabeth sighed. "Well . . ." She tapped her pencil against her pad. "Our dorm rooms are too small. And it's too late to reserve a large enough space at a restaurant."

"What about Steven and Billie's apartment?"

Elizabeth took another bite of her taco. "I thought about that. But Billie told me she's going to be home all day, so there's no way I can sneak in to set up."

Tom leaned back in his chair. "Let me see that list again. One of these people must have the answer."

Elizabeth handed it over, and Tom started to read out loud. "You and me, Jessica and . . ."

A tap at the window startled her. Elizabeth looked up and all the pieces fell into place. "Mike McAllery!" she exclaimed. She waved for Mike to join them.

Tom nodded. "Exactly."

Mike entered the Mexican Café and straddled the seat between Elizabeth and Tom. "What's up?" he asked. "Mind if I . . ." He grabbed a tortilla chip

67

and popped it into his mouth. "Great news about Steven and Billie."

Elizabeth gave Tom a conspiratorial wink. "Sure is. Such great news, I thought we should have a party to celebrate."

Mike nodded. "Yeah, I'd be in on that."

Tom held out the basket of tortilla chips. "Have another."

Elizabeth pushed over the guacamole. "Only problem is, we don't know where to have it."

Mike smirked. "Give me the time and the date, and my place is yours."

Elizabeth laughed. "That's great, Mike. Thanks. I thought that if we had it tonight, we would really catch them off guard."

"No problem," Mike said. "I even have party hats left over from New Year's Eve."

Elizabeth grinned. She hadn't thought of party hats. That would be a special touch. "Jess and I will come over later to decorate and make some food."

"Jess makes great guacamole," Mike said, sounding a little wistful.

Elizabeth looked up and smiled happily. Mike wasn't such a bad guy behind that gruff exterior. He had really helped out Steven. And if she wasn't mistaken, there was still a gleam in his eye for Jessica.

Mike smiled with amusement as he watched Jessica gracefully bustle around his kitchen. She might not be much of a cook, but she sure looked good. Her satiny golden hair was wound in a tight French twist that exposed the back of her long, delicate neck. Mike felt his heart begin to hammer as the strap of her pale violet dress slipped a notch, revealing a glimpse of slim, tanned shoulder. He ruefully shook his head. He had to admit that Jessica Wakefield still had a powerful effect on him.

Elizabeth poked her head into the kitchen. "I've got to run to the store and get Steven and Billie's engagement cake. Do you two need anything?"

"No," Mike answered quickly. He was happy for the opportunity to be alone with Jessica. "Unless you need something, Jess?" he asked.

She shook her head and sliced into a tomato. "I'm just fine," she said in a clipped tone.

"I could make you a drink," he offered after Elizabeth had left. He knew how she loved seltzer with a splash of cranberry juice.

"No, thank you," she said, reaching into his utensil drawer and pulling out a vegetable peeler. She started to work on a large, ripe avocado.

For a moment as he watched her, his apron tied around her waist, it felt as if she'd never left. If it weren't for her glaring at him every time their eyes met, this could almost be like old times.

"Could you get that bowl down, please?" Jessica asked.

"Sure," Mike said, reaching up to get a big serving bowl he kept on the top shelf. "You never could reach those."

"Then I guess next time you'll be better off with a taller woman," Jessica said curtly, pushing back a loose wisp of her blond hair. "Oh, but Val Tripler's almost five foot nine, so I guess you've already solved that problem."

69

Mike frowned. He wasn't going to touch that remark with a ten-foot pole.

Jessica dumped the peeled and pitted avocados along with the tomatoes into the bowl and began violently smashing the concoction with a fork.

Mike raised his eyebrows. It wasn't exactly the way he would do it. But hey, she was the cook. He opened a bag of tortilla chips and snaked his hand around her side to steal a taste.

"Stop it!" she yelled, slapping his hand. "That's for tonight."

"It needs some chili pepper," Mike said, reaching for the spice bottle.

"No, it doesn't," Jessica snapped. "You'll ruin it. Like you've ruined everything else."

Mike took a step back. So far they'd only made onion dip and that had come out pretty well. "Hey, I'm just trying to help."

Jessica turned toward him, her face contorted in anger. "You have a funny way of helping," she hissed. "And it always comes down to what's best for Mike McAllery."

"Jess," Mike said helplessly. "I thought the guacamole was a little bland. Most people like it with a kick."

"If you think that's what I'm talking about," Jessica snarled, slamming down the bowl, "then you're even more thickheaded than I thought."

Mike shrugged. "If you're trying to say something, Jess, say it. Please. Before you break all my dishes."

Jessica took a deep breath.

He could tell she was about to unload on him with both barrels.

"You told Val that she should break up her partnership with me so I could concentrate on school," she said accusingly.

Mike nodded—that was exactly right.

Jessica's eyes widened. "That's a total lie!" she screamed. "You want Val and me to split up so you can have her all to yourself. Admit it."

"Jessica," Mike said, reaching out to calm her down. "That's not true."

"Don't touch me," Jessica shrieked. "I know about you and Val. You're afraid we'll start comparing notes. And you can't take that chance. So you'd rather throw me out of my career, my chance of success, than risk her finding out what a loser you are."

Mike shook his head. This was getting totally out of hand. Part of him wanted to say forget it. Why should he waste his breath trying to defend himself when he'd already been tried and convicted? But sensing the hurt behind Jessica's anger, he resolved to give it one more go.

"Jessica," Mike said as patiently as he could. "Val's already made it. She's been working in the fashion business for five years. She knows her stuff." He shrugged. "You're starting out. You were successful this time, but who knows about next time. You don't have any training or any foundation."

"In case you hadn't noticed," Jessica said damply, "most of Val's success came from having a very supportive backer. Something I certainly don't have."

"Backer or no backer," Mike began.

"No," Jessica said, rudely cutting him off. "If I had the kind of supportive, pro-Jessica type of person in my corner that Val has—someone with faith in me and vision, someone who trusted my sense and abilities, who didn't put me down every five minutes and laugh at the mere thought of me doing anything—I could go far in this field too."

Mike grabbed his head. "If you'd listen to me for five seconds—" He wanted to explain to her what was going on.

Jessica stamped her foot. "Stop trying to interrupt me. Val is the luckiest person in the world. I don't know who her backer is, but I wish I had someone like that." Her eyes steamed. "All I have is you, trying to ruin what little success I've got."

Mike watched helplessly as she stormed out of the apartment, slamming the front door behind her. His head was spinning. She'd done it again. Twisted all his words and all his attempts to help into something bad. He was sick of being treated like the villain when he'd done nothing wrong. Trying to help Jessica was a thankless task. If she refused to see that he'd changed, then fine. He'd go back to being the old Mike. Back to being the baddest guy in town.

He reached for the phone. The first order of business for the old Mike was to line up a date for tonight. He thumbed through his little black book until he came to *R*. *R* as in redheads, like the girl he'd seen the other night at the Last Stop Bar. With any luck she'd be free to take him up on that rain check.

"Surprise!"

Billie gasped as the lights snapped on in Mike McAllery's darkened apartment, freezing her and Steven in the doorway. She had a half second to think *surprise party!* and then all of their friends rushed forward at once, hugging and patting them on the back.

"Congratulations!"

"Great news!"

Mike's apartment was decked out in full party gear. Streamers hung from the ceiling. Everyone was wearing a party hat. People were blowing noisemakers and shouting. It was New Year's Eve in April!

"Mike, I'm going to get you for this," she heard Steven say over the pounding in her chest. Her heart was going a mile a minute.

Mike held up his hands. "Don't blame me. Better talk to Elizabeth and Jess." He slapped Steven on the back and gave Billie a big hug.

Jessica and Elizabeth ran up and Billie laughed and hugged them too as they positioned one of the party hats on her head.

"You guys," Billie said, beaming. "I should have guessed." Mike had sounded so serious on the phone that she'd actually been afraid something terrible had happened. The last thing on her mind had been a surprise engagement party. Especially on such short notice.

"Let's start the music and boogie," Winston yelled, waving his arms over his head and shaking his body.

Not just a surprise party, Billie thought, *a surprise dance party.* The living-room furniture had been pushed against the wall to open up a makeshift dance floor.

Winston's girlfriend, Denise, giggled and leapt up to join him. Danny flipped on the stereo and did a moonwalk into the center of the living room as Isabella shimmied after him. Then the whole room seemed to explode into dancing. Bruce was spinning Lila around in a circle, and Noah and Alexandra were shaking it for all they were worth. Then Winston cleared the floor, shifting gears into some of his legendary break-dance moves.

"How does he do that?" Elizabeth asked over Billie's shoulder. "It looks like he's made of rubber."

"Amazing," Billie said, and then turned to Elizabeth and gave her another hug. "This whole party is amazing. Thanks for setting it up for us."

"Our pleasure," Elizabeth said. "Even if you guys weren't getting married, seeing you back together calls for a celebration."

Billie smiled, feeling great. Everyone seemed as excited about her and Steven getting back together as she was. She couldn't have wished for better friends. *Or better future sisters-in-law,* she thought.

"Hey, Mrs. Wakefield-to-be," Steven said, coming up behind her and putting his arms around her waist. "How about we show these guys how to really dance?"

Billie laughed and fell into Steven's strong arms. He hugged her tight and they started a slow, close dance, ignoring the thumping beat of the music blasting from the stereo.

"Mr. Wakefield," she said, looking up from his chest. "Have I told you I loved you recently?"

"Not for the past ten minutes," Steven said.

"Well, I do," she whispered.

"Just keep that 'I do' in mind this weekend," Steven said.

Billie smiled and snuggled closer to him. Soon Tom and Elizabeth glided past, doing their own slow dance. Billie raised her head from Steven's chest and looked around. Alexandra and Noah had entwined themselves in each other's arms and were swaying back and forth. Even Bruce and Lila had stopped spinning and were holding each other close. Everyone was ignoring the fast tempo of the music.

She smiled at the thought of this thoroughly modern group shuffling the old two-step, clinging to each other like dancers from the black-and-white movies of the 1930s.

Billie sighed and murmured into Steven's ear, "Do you think it's catching?"

Steven turned his head to see the other couples embracing. "Love?" he whispered. "It sure looks like it."

Billie closed her eyes and held Steven tight as someone hit the CD changer. Soon Frank Sinatra was crooning "Strangers in the Night" to the room full of slow dancers.

"Steven," she said with a giggle, "I think we're turning into our parents."

Jessica stood alone in a corner of Mike's living room, watching the couples swaying on the dance floor. *Everyone except me is having a great time,* she thought. *It's not fair.* This was supposed to be a celebration of Steven and Billie's engagement. Jessica had imagined a big, lively party, full of people laughing and having fun. Instead the party was turning into a couple's convention. *And I'm the odd woman out,* she thought.

All this slow dancing was enough to make her nauseous. Worst of all, the one person who could have been her partner was now spinning a stunning redhead in a tight black cocktail dress around the room.

"As far as Mike's concerned," she said to herself, "I'm right where I belong. Pushed to one side with the rest of the furniture while he has a great time."

Jessica sniffed and adjusted the hem of her own little black dress. It wasn't as tight or low cut as the redhead's. *But,* she thought, tossing back her blond head in her freshly coiled French twist, *I have more style.*

Jessica glanced over to see what Val thought of Mike's dance partner. But she was deep in conversation with one of Billie and Steven's neighbors. She didn't seem the least bit concerned.

Mercifully the music stopped, and Jessica watched as the couples broke apart. All except Mike and the redhead. The woman kept swaying against him.

"Someone should tell her the song is over," Jessica scoffed under her breath. "That or remove the Walkman from her brain."

Jessica turned as Steven tapped a spoon against his glass. "I'd like to make a toast," he said when the room had quieted down. "Billie and I want to take this moment to tell you what a great group of friends you are. And if we ever get over the fright you gave us, we just might thank you for this party, too."

The room broke into laughter.

"Only kidding," Steven said. "We really appreciate everything you've done for us. You guys believed in us even when we were having doubts. Thanks for being there."

Jessica joined in the cheering. A chorus of noise-makers started up again. *This is more like it,* she thought. Maybe this party was going to turn into a celebration after all.

"One more thing," Steven said. "I want to make a special toast to a guy who really helped me. He took me in while Billie and I worked things out. And as you know, that was at a serious risk to his own reputation." Steven laughed. "To my great pal and, if he'll do me the honor, my future best man, Mike McAllery."

The room exploded in applause, but Jessica couldn't believe her ears. Mike McAllery, best man? As one of Billie's maids of honor that meant she'd have to walk down the aisle with him. *No way!* Jessica thought. She'd made that mistake once before. She wasn't going to do it again.

Mike and Steven were still slapping each other on the back as she pushed through the crowd. Enough was enough. She stepped in front of her brother.

"If you think I'm going to be part of any wedding that *he's* in, you're crazy," she said, her voice catching on the knot in her throat. "Count me out!"

She blindly ran for the door. She wasn't going to let the whole room see her cry. She ignored Billie, Elizabeth, and everything else but her main objective: to get out of there and be as far away from everybody as she could. She headed for the stairs.

Outside, the soft evening air cooled the hot tears that were running down her cheeks. Stars twinkled in the velvet blanket of the night sky above her. She listened in the stillness, suddenly hearing another set of footsteps on the stairs from Mike's apartment. She quickly started walking away, making it as far as the parking lot before Val caught up with her.

Jessica turned. "Leave me alone, Val."

"Listen to me," Val said, grabbing her arms. "Stop acting like a baby and listen."

"No," Jessica cried. "I've heard enough and I've seen enough. I know what's going on."

"No, you don't," Val said. "You find out a few bits and pieces and then you think you know the whole story. Well, you're wrong this time, so you'd better listen to what's right."

Jessica shook her head. If Val wasn't holding her arms, she would put her hands up to her ears and cover them.

"Listen," Val ordered, shaking her. "You want to know what's going on between me and Mike, so I'll tell you. Mike was a friend of my husband, Derek."

Jessica looked up. Val had been married?

"Derek was a race-car driver. He and Mike met while Mike was trying to break into semipro racing. Three years ago Derek's car was caught in a pileup at the Santa Clara raceway. He was in a coma for days. When he died, part of me died with him."

Val paused. Even in the darkness of the parking lot, Jessica could see that her eyes were brimming with tears.

"Mike was there for me every step of the way. That's the kind of person he is. He arranged the funeral, did everything. We kept in touch after I went back east to go to design school. When I came here and started working at Taylor's Department Store, I called him. And when you started working there, Mike asked me to keep an eye on you. That's how you and I became friends."

Jessica's mouth dropped open. "Mike asked you to look out for me?"

"Wake up, Jessica," Val said. "Mike's been watching out for you this whole time. It was Mike who put up the money to save our business when the warehouse burned down. He sold that beautiful vintage Mustang to do it."

Jessica shook her head dumbly. Mike had been Val's mysterious backer? *And hers!*

"To help *you*," Jessica argued. "He didn't want *your* chance at success to be ruined." But even as she said the words, she knew that wasn't how it had happened. Everything Val had said rang true.

Val shook her head. "No," she said firmly. "He did it for you. Mike wouldn't have sold his prize car for me. But for you he would, Jessica. I'm going back to the party. I hope you come to your senses."

Jessica watched, stunned, as Val walked away, her words echoing in Jessica's mind. *For you, Jessica. He did it for you.* But why? If Mike still cared about her, still loved her, then why hadn't he said so? *Maybe he has been saying so, Jess,* she thought. *Maybe he's been saying so all along and you just haven't been listening.*

*   *   *

Tom and Elizabeth parted after a long, deep kiss on the stone steps outside Dickenson Hall, the modern, glass-faced tower that housed Elizabeth's dorm. Tom could have stood there kissing her for hours. It was a beautiful night. *But Elizabeth must be tired,* he reminded himself. She'd been working all day to get Billie and Steven's surprise engagement party organized.

"Great party," he whispered. "Steven and Billie are lucky to have someone like you around. And so am I," he added.

"Thanks," Elizabeth said, smiling up at him. Even her bright blue-green eyes couldn't hide her sleepiness. "Now about tomorrow . . ."

Tom had been dreading this subject since they'd left Mike's apartment and headed for Elizabeth's dorm. In the morning everyone was heading out to Sweet Valley to help get the Wakefields' house ready for the wedding.

Tom leaned against the thin metal railing that ran along the steps. "I'm not so sure about tomorrow, Liz. I was thinking I might not come until the ceremony."

"What?" Elizabeth asked. "Why?"

Tom traced his finger along the railing's cool metal and stared down at his black high-tops. "I feel funny about being there." He shrugged. "I don't know anything about weddings. I'm afraid I'll be in the way."

"Don't worry about that," Elizabeth said with a laugh. "That's my mother's department."

Tom ran a hand through his dark brown hair. He didn't want to have to remind Elizabeth how

80

much they'd fought the last time Billie and Steven were supposed to get married.

Elizabeth sighed and leaned against the other side of the railing, the light from the large glass entrance illuminating her golden hair. "I know what you're thinking, and you're right. It's going to be a zoo. People are going to be running around like maniacs. My sister and mother will probably be at each other's throats. But I have to be there."

Tom looked off across the darkened campus. Only a few rooms remained lighted. A few lonely souls burning the midnight oil. Wouldn't he be one of them with Elizabeth gone? Definitely.

"It's not that I don't want to be with you," Tom said. "But all that activity makes me crazy."

Elizabeth smiled. "Me too," she said. "That's why I need you around. To keep me sane. You've met my mother. You've seen how she gets. She's trying to create the perfect wedding in less than a week when any normal person would need a year."

"Oh, is that right, Ms. Surprise-Party-in-a-Day Wakefield?"

Elizabeth giggled, and he took her in his arms. He looked down at her face, lingering on the tender curve of her smile. There was only one thing he wanted to do less than go to Sweet Valley tomorrow and that was disappoint Elizabeth.

"Okay," Tom said. "I'll go. But let's promise not to fight. No matter how crazy things get."

"It's a deal," Elizabeth said, her beautiful blue-green eyes shining with happiness. "It might even be fun."

Tom groaned. "I'll be happy if we can get through it in one piece."

Jessica walked slowly through the warm, balmy night back toward the SVU campus. She had been walking around for what seemed like hours. Her tears had dried, but her thoughts were still a mass of confusion. *Mike was our backer,* she thought again. He'd been helping Jessica, *not* hurting her all along. *And Mike and Val aren't going out, either,* she thought. *I was wrong about that, too.* A small smile played on her lips.

She'd reached the large, deserted academic quad when another memory popped into her brain. This time she winced, remembering her threat to boycott Steven and Billie's wedding if Mike was in it. She stopped, knowing she had to talk to Mike before she went to sleep. She wasn't sure whether she was going to condemn him, apologize to him, or thank him. But she had to do something. She had to tell him that she knew he'd been her and Val's backer *and* find out why he'd kept it from her.

But I look awful, she thought. The French twist she'd carefully arranged before the party had come completely undone. She could feel how swollen her eyes were from crying. Even her smart black party dress was wrinkled beyond recognition. *It doesn't matter,* she told herself. Jessica turned and started back toward Mike's.

She'd expected to hear music and loud laughter as she approached Mike's apartment building. But from outside, there was only silence. She opened the door and crept up the darkened staircase. Only the sliver of light from under Mike's door kept her walking down the hall. He opened the door to her third knock, a roll of paper towels tucked under his arm and two crushed soda cans in his left hand.

She expected a snide comment about her appearance, but there was none. "The party's over," he said flatly. His eyes seemed guarded and his mouth taut.

Jessica hesitated before taking a step closer. "I know you sold the Mustang," she whispered. "Val told me you were our backer."

Mike nodded and pushed the door all the way open for her to come in.

Jessica stepped over a bulging green garbage bag and looked around the living room for a seat. The furniture was still pushed aside against the walls. She walked over and perched on the arm of his black leather couch.

"I can move that back for you," Mike offered.

Jessica shook her head. "I won't be here that long." She looked up at him, her eyes narrowed suspiciously. "Why didn't you tell me? Why were you being so secretive?"

Mike shrugged and emptied an ashtray in the garbage bag. "I tried to tell you this afternoon when you were making the guacamole. But you wouldn't let me."

Jessica tossed her loose golden hair over her shoulder. "That was this afternoon. You've been our backer for weeks."

Mike sighed and turned toward her. "At the time it seemed easier. I didn't think you'd trust me. I was afraid you wouldn't accept my help."

Jessica's eyes darkened. *He was right*, she thought. After all the pain and misunderstanding between them, she might have refused his help.

"I'm sorry," Mike said. "I shouldn't have kept you in the dark. I should have offered to help and let you make the decision. Like your choice between staying in business with Val and concentrating on school. I promise I won't try to interfere in that again."

Jessica felt her eyes begin to well up for the second time that night. She smiled. "Thank you, Mike. But the truth is, I appreciated your advice. I've come to the conclusion that you and Val are right. It *is* too soon for me to give up school and go into business full time. Right now I need to concentrate on college. You helped me to see that."

Mike stepped toward her, his golden eyes soft in the diffuse glow of the living room's track lighting. "Can we call a truce? Try and be friends?"

What could she say now, after everything that had happened between them? One tear spilled down Jessica's cheek.

He cupped her face and wiped the tear away. "Please, Jess, give me another chance. Give *us* another chance. . . ."

"Us?" Jessica felt her body melting against his, but at the same time her mind flashed on some of the hurtful episodes from their past. "I don't want to get hurt again," she said, drawing back from him. "I couldn't take that."

"Can't we forget the past?" Mike whispered. "Can't we start over and try to get it right this time?"

"I'm scared," Jessica said.

"So am I. But I'll risk it if you will."

Jessica nodded. "We'll have to go slow."

"Okay," Mike said. "Tell you what. We're all going to be in Sweet Valley helping Billie and Steven get ready for the wedding, right? How about if you and I go out then? I'll pick you up at your parents' house. It will be a regular, proper date."

"With a chaperone?" Jessica teased, her tears forgotten.

"If you want," Mike said solemnly. "But," he added, putting his hand behind his back, "I promise I'll be on my best behavior even without one."

Jessica craned her neck. "I see those crossed fingers."

Mike laughed and pulled her toward him. "For real. I promise."

Chapter
Five

"What a great morning for a drive," Bruce said to himself as he walked across the parking lot. Everyone was meeting to drive, caravan style, to the Wakefields' house in Sweet Valley. The warm California sun was shining brightly in the sky. Fresh dew was glistening on the grass, on the SVU dorm windows, and, he thought with a deep sigh, on the windshield of his shiny, fire-engine-red Jeep Grand Cherokee.

Bruce opened the Cherokee's door and took a yellow buff rag from his glove compartment. He blotted lovingly at the Jeep's moist surface. Some people might think he was obsessive about his car, but he was just looking after his investment.

"Yo, Patman," Winston called, coming out of his dorm. "It's only water, you know. That stuff dries all by itself. It's called evaporation. You should look into it."

"You wouldn't know it, looking at your car,"

Bruce yelled back, giving the hood a last wipe. Winston's old VW Bug was an eyesore. The floor was practically rusted straight through.

Bruce turned at the sound of a horn honking. It was Elizabeth, Jessica, and Tom pulling up in the twins' Jeep.

"Hey," Bruce called to them. "Where's Lila? I thought she was riding with you."

Jessica leaned forward from the backseat. "Haven't seen her. She told me last night if she wasn't here by eight, we should go without her."

Bruce groaned. That meant Lila had probably overslept. If the twins left and he was out here when Lila came down, she would expect him to drive her to Sweet Valley and be her chauffeur their whole time there. But he couldn't. He had an important appointment to keep day after tomorrow. And if there was one person he couldn't have tagging along, it was Lila.

Bruce grimaced as the twins' Jeep began pulling away. Fortunately they stopped a few yards farther down the parking lot to talk to Alexandra, who was getting into Noah's convertible.

Bruce jumped into his Cherokee. It was now or never. If he left before the twins, Lila could hardly blame him for not having given her a lift. Maybe she'd even take her own car, which would really get him off the hook. He revved the engine and threw the Cherokee into reverse. Usually he gave the motor a good five minutes to warm up, but this would have to be an exception.

He backed smoothly out of his parking spot and was just about to pull forward when Winston suddenly began backing out too, cutting Bruce off.

So close, Bruce thought, banging his steering wheel horn. He sat there helplessly as Winston's bomb spluttered and coughed, finally chugging its way out of the parking space. Bruce looked up to see the twins leaving them in the dust, their Jeep shooting off in the direction of the highway.

"Hurry up, Winston," Bruce cried. "Go. Go! If Lila comes out here, I'm cooked."

Winston's car stalled out. Bruce groaned and dropped his head onto the steering wheel. He'd never get away now. Lila would find him. She'd insist on their going to Sweet Valley together.

He jumped as the passenger door opened. Sure enough, Lila slid in beside him, wearing a sleek black pantsuit and clutching a small red handbag.

"Lucky I caught you," Lila said. "These shoes aren't exactly made for walking." She displayed a pair of formidable black sling-back heels. "Where's the fire?"

Bruce gulped. "I thought you were going with Jessica and Liz."

"Changed my mind," Lila said. "But I didn't expect you to be running off this early."

"I have a lot of errands to run," he offered, trying to sound casual. "Figured I'd get an early start." He didn't dare mention his appointment in two days.

Lila slipped a pair of designer tortoiseshell sunglasses out of her handbag and put them on. She turned Bruce's rearview mirror toward her, checking her fashionable reflection. "As a matter of fact, I have some errands to run myself."

Bruce's stomach sank. Now he really was stuck. Knowing Lila, she'd insist on their running their errands together. He would have to reschedule his appointment for after Billie and Steven's wedding.

Winston's car started up again, backfired, and then puttered off in the direction of the highway.

"Okay, your ladyship," he said. "Where to?"

"Make a right," Lila said.

Bruce frowned. That was the way back to campus.

Lila reached into her handbag again, extracting the keys to her jet-black Miata. "I told you I had errands to run." She jingled the shiny keys in the air and shrugged her slender shoulders. "Naturally I need my car in Sweet Valley if I'm going to run them. I need *you* to drive me over to my car. It's in the other lot."

"No problem," Bruce said, resisting the urge to laugh. He sat a little straighter in his seat. "Always happy to be of service."

"Hey, buddy," Mike said, opening his apartment door. Before him stood a slightly disheveled Steven Wakefield. "I thought you'd be on your way to Sweet Valley by now."

"Almost," Steven said, tucking in his pin-striped oxford shirt. "But I wanted to talk to you before Billie and I headed out."

"Come on in," Mike said, stepping back. "Do you want coffee?"

"Sure," Steven said. "I'm only going to have time for about two sips, though. Billie's about packed and my mother's already called ten times. She's arranged a tux fitting for me this morning."

Mike led Steven into the kitchen and poured them each a steaming mug of coffee. They stood at the barlike counter in the center of the room.

"So . . . you're really going through with it," Mike said, passing Steven the milk. "Tired of bachelor life already."

Steven grinned. "I wasn't very good at it, was I?"

"Not really." Mike chuckled, thinking of the ripped felt on the Last Stop's pool table. "Though I can think of a couple of bar owners who'll sleep more soundly from now on."

"Hey," Steven said, "I told them I'd pay for that pool table felt. They're supposed to give me an estimate on the price."

"A pair of broken kneecaps, most likely," Mike said, straight-faced.

Steven's mouth dropped. But then he broke into a grin. "Get out of here," he said. "I'm finally catching on to your sense of humor, McAllery." He feigned a punch to Mike's midsection.

Mike laughed and crouched into a fighter's stance. "About time, my man," he said. He turned and opened the refrigerator. "Can I get you something to eat? There's enough food left over from the party to last a lifetime."

"Tempting," Steven said. "But we really have to go. I stopped by to say thanks for last night. Billie and I had a great time."

"Me too," Mike said. "Course, Elizabeth and Jessica did all the work. Oh yeah, by the way, Jess and I called a truce last night. Her boycott of the wedding is off, in case she didn't mention it."

Steven shook his head. "Good. I'm glad she

91

chilled out. She can really drive you insane once she gets an idea in her head."

"Tell me about it," Mike said. He'd never met a woman who'd caused him more trouble. But then, he'd never felt about a woman the way he felt about Jessica, either.

Steven took a sip of his coffee. "So when are you coming down?" he asked. "My mother's already setting up a spare room for you."

Whoa! The Wakefields' house was not on Mike's list of potential accommodations for the big wedding weekend.

"Uh, that's okay," Mike said. "You don't have to do that. You'll have plenty of people to put up without worrying about me."

Steven leaned against the counter. "It's no problem, really. You're the best man, after all. As far as I'm concerned that makes you a top priority."

Mike shook his head. "Thanks, but I'll grab a hotel room. Nothing personal, but being around parent types sort of makes me . . ."

Steven laughed and put down his mug. "I get it. The whole authority thing."

Mike nodded. He'd been on his own since he was sixteen. The thought of someone's mother clucking over him to make sure he cleared his plate or someone's father checking the clock when he rolled in past midnight was not his idea of a good time.

"If you change your mind," Steven said, walking to the door, "let me know. Bedrooms are a hot commodity at our place for the next few days."

"Don't worry about me," Mike said. "I'll call

you when I get settled into my hotel." Roughly speaking, he estimated the chance of his changing his mind at about a trillion to one.

Tom leaned back in the Jeep's passenger seat and watched the world speed by. Elizabeth was driving while Jessica bounced up and down in back to a song on the radio. He still wasn't sure if his going to Sweet Valley to help with the wedding preparations was the best idea. *But at least I'll be with Liz,* he thought.

Elizabeth signaled and cut smoothly across two lanes of traffic. "Detour," she said. "I thought we'd take the coast for a few miles."

Tom raised his eyebrows. He'd been to the Wakefields' house a couple of times before but always by the freeway.

Elizabeth made an abrupt right turn and then two quick lefts. Suddenly the world seemed to slip away and the Jeep was alone on a skinny road, high up in the cliffs, racing along the Pacific coastline.

Tom's eyes widened. The ocean lay below them, its magnificent blue waves crashing against the shore. Whitecaps dominated the surface, and he longed for a surfboard and a wet suit.

"That's gorgeous." Tom whistled. "I had no idea."

Elizabeth smiled, her eyes shining. "I knew you'd like this," she said. "This is my favorite stretch of road in the whole world."

"You've never been here?" Jessica asked, sitting forward between the two front seats. "This is the prettiest route to take when you're leaving campus."

Tom nodded, mesmerized by the violence of the

rumbling surf. "I don't do much traveling."

"Well, next time you're going somewhere," Jessica said, "in the summertime or school holidays, take this route. The stretch going north is just as nice. You can—"

"I'll remember that," Tom interrupted sharply. He winced. He hadn't meant to be rude to Jessica, but the truth was he had no place to go. When the other students went home for school holidays or visits with their parents, Tom stayed on campus. He had no family to visit.

Elizabeth reached over and squeezed his hand. She was the only person who knew how he felt about the accident that had killed his family. For a long time, he'd blamed himself for their deaths. He'd been doing his big-man-on-campus act and had selfishly insisted that his family make the long drive from Colorado to SVU to see him play in a football game. They'd never made it. Instead his father had lost control of the family minivan on one of the icy mountain roads on the way. His father, mother, older sister, and younger brother had all died in the crash.

It was Elizabeth's love that had finally gotten him over the guilt he'd felt and helped his heart to heal. Elizabeth, his roommate, Danny, and his other friends at SVU were his family now.

"I wish you were staying with us," Elizabeth said.

Jessica sat forward again. "Isn't he?"

Elizabeth shook her head. "No. Mom's reserved all the rooms for out-of-town relatives."

"That figures." Jessica groaned. "Not only is she

going to try and run the whole wedding, she's going to dominate the guest list as well." Jessica let out a loud sigh. "So where are you staying, Tom?"

"With Winston's family," Tom said.

"Uh-oh." Jessica smirked. "They live down the street. I know a couple who must be planning a midnight rendezvous or two."

"That's more your department, Jess," Elizabeth said sternly.

Tom laughed. "While under the Egberts' roof, I've promised to follow the Egberts' rules."

"That may be harder than you think," Jessica said. "Mr. and Mrs. Egbert make our parents look soft. Though you're probably better off. If I know Mom, she'll be handing out long lists of horrible tasks for each of us to do as soon as we get home."

"Don't listen to her," Elizabeth countered. "Mom is not going to do that."

"She is so," Jessica cut in.

Elizabeth rolled her eyes. "And the Egberts are perfectly nice," she continued. "Look at Winston. How bad can they be?"

There was a moment's hesitation and then they all burst out laughing.

Elizabeth pulled off the coast road and threaded back into freeway traffic. Tom closed his eyes as the stark beauty of the coastline was replaced by honking motorists and modern shopping centers. He smiled slightly to himself. *This might not be so bad after all,* he thought. It had been a long time, a very long time, since he'd been in the company of a real family. Even if Jessica was right and Winston's parents were strict, he didn't mind. It would be home life, after all. Something that, even though he had Elizabeth and all his SVU friends, he still missed.

Any second now and I'm going to turn this radio up to ten! Elizabeth thought, gritting her teeth. Anything to drown out Jessica's griping about their mother. The closer to their parents' house on Calico Drive they got, the worse it was becoming. Jessica was rapidly approaching a full-scale whining fit.

Jessica sat forward and practically yelled in her ear, "I don't see why it doesn't bother you, Liz. Mom's going to push you around too."

"So what's the use?" Elizabeth asked. She crossed over to the slow lane to let a speeding car pass by. "You know what's going to happen. You know how Mom is. Why don't you just accept it and deal with it?"

Elizabeth bit her lower lip as she caught Jessica's furious look in the rearview mirror. She'd meant to keep out of it, but Jessica's ranting about their mother's bossiness and how she was going to control the whole wedding was getting to her.

"Aren't you sick of it?" Jessica asked bitterly, flinging herself against the backseat. "She treats us like we're infants. I have ideas too. My fashion and design sense is every bit as good as hers."

Elizabeth caught Tom's eye and gave him an exasperated look. "It's her house, Jess. When you're the mother and you have children getting married, then you can run the show."

"That's ridiculous," Jessica wailed. "It should be

a joint effort. Don't you think so, Tom?"

Elizabeth glanced over at him as he shrugged. He was wisely keeping out of it. "Jess, why don't you calm down?"

"Why should I?" she snapped. "I'm sick of being ordered around like I don't have a brain in my head. Remember when I was looking for material for our maid-of-honor dresses? Nothing was good enough for her. And you know why those fabrics weren't 'appropriate,' as she kept saying? Because I picked them out. If she'd spotted any one of those fabrics first, you can bet Val would be making dresses out of them right now."

"What are you getting at?" Elizabeth asked. She slowed down to let in a car that was pulling off the shoulder.

"It's me," Jessica fumed. "She didn't like the fabric because I picked it out."

Elizabeth made a face. She checked her side mirror and then eased into the middle lane.

Tom turned in his seat to look at Jessica. "Now you're sounding paranoid."

"No," Jessica stated flatly. "I'm not paranoid. It would have been the same thing if Liz had picked it out, and she knows it. It's Mom. It's only okay if she does it."

Elizabeth shook her head. *Like mother, like daughter,* she thought. She had only to remember the decoration of their dorm room to see the similarities. Jessica had vetoed everything Elizabeth had wanted to do. If Elizabeth hadn't finally put her foot down, every poster on the wall, the bedspreads, and the curtains on the windows would have been Jessica's choice. She glanced over at Tom again. Good grief. This was going to be like World War III. She hoped he was up for it.

"You're running low on gas," Tom said.

Elizabeth gave a start. She'd been so wrapped up in her and Jessica's family drama that she hadn't even noticed. She exited the highway at the next service station.

"I'll get us sodas," Jessica said, stepping out of the Jeep. "Diet colas okay?"

"Sure," Elizabeth said. Tom was already outside, fiddling with the gas pump.

"You gallant man," Elizabeth said, coming up behind him. "I can do that."

"I needed a breather," Tom said.

Elizabeth winced. "I'm sorry. I'm glad you and I pledged not to fight. I wish I could say the same for Jess and my mother."

"I'm sure it can't be as bad as Jess makes out."

Elizabeth sighed. "I'm afraid it might be worse. Sometimes I think they're total opposites. But when it comes to bossiness, they're carbon copies."

Tom let out a low whistle. "Then this should be interesting."

Elizabeth grimaced. "Unfortunately one of my major jobs will be to run interference between them. I hope it won't be too terrible for you."

"I'll manage," Tom said. "I've already promised myself that no matter what, I'm not going to get caught up in any Wakefield family fireworks. Let them fight all they want. I'm unflappable."

Elizabeth laughed. "Brave man." She wished she could say the same for herself.

*   *   *

"Yoo-hoo! Bride and groom!" Mrs. Wakefield's cheerful voice called out across the expansive yard. "The minister will be here any minute to discuss the ceremony. You'd better come inside."

Billie sighed. The birds had barely woken up and begun their early morning warbling and already the duties of the day were starting. Even from a distance of a hundred feet, she could feel the Wakefields' house humming. With the wedding only three days away, every square inch of the place was buzzing with activity. This morning every room seemed to be filled with people. She'd had to lead Steven to the furthest reaches of the backyard, ducking under trees and squeezing between the thick shrubs, so they could share a moment of peace together. *But even this isn't far enough,* she thought.

"Oh, well," Steven said. "Duty calls."

"Hold on—I think a little rehearsal is in order first," Billie teased. She put her arms around him and stole one last kiss before they slowly walked toward the back door.

Denise and Isabella ran past them, giggling, practically knocking Billie over as she stepped into the hallway.

"Are they staying here too?" she asked Steven, exasperated.

Steven laughed and pulled her toward him. "No. It just feels that way. They're staying with Alexandra." He nodded to the right. "Next-door neighbors. I think my mom has them on the decoration committee."

Billie grimaced. *It's not funny,* she thought. It was her wedding, but it seemed more like a prolonged house party for the twins and their friends.

"With all this commotion I can barely think," she complained.

Steven shrugged. "Get used to it. More people are planning to come over this afternoon."

Billie shook her head. It was sweet of Elizabeth and Jessica to offer their friends' services, but this was getting out of hand. She'd thought she and Steven would have *some* quiet time with the family. But since they'd arrived yesterday afternoon, it had been one crowd scene after another. With friends outnumbering Wakefields three to one, she almost wished she and Steven had stayed home and only showed up for the ceremony. *Better yet,* she thought, *why couldn't all the guests have stayed home until then?*

The doorbell rang, and Mrs. Wakefield ushered in the minister, a very old, slightly stooped man who wore dark slacks and a tidy black shirt. His traditional white collar matched the shock of white hair on his head. He moved slowly toward her and Steven.

Oh no, Billie thought. *He looks about a hundred. How's he going to deal with all this wedding madness?*

"Billie," Mrs. Wakefield said, taking the minister's jacket, "this is the Reverend Alan Dexter. He was Steven and the twins' Sunday-school teacher."

Billie smiled and held out her hand. The elderly man was just reaching out to shake hers when Tom and Winston stormed through the front door, arms laden with Chinese lanterns. The minister stumbled back, looking frightened.

I hope all this activity isn't going to unnerve him too badly, she thought.

"Why don't we do this in the dining room?" Steven suggested, leading the way. "I'm afraid the rest of the house is a bit of a zoo."

"Understandable," the minister said softly. "A few visitors, I suppose?"

That's the understatement of the year, Billie thought, but kept it to herself.

When they were settled around the dining-room table, the minister opened his briefcase and took out a notepad. "Let me see if I have the facts right." He adjusted a pair of ancient wire-rimmed spectacles on his long, thin nose. "I like to mention a few personal details in my sermon."

He thumbed through his notebook until he got to the right page. "Steven Wakefield and Billie Winkler."

A loud crash came from the kitchen. The minister looked up nervously.

"Don't mind that," Steven said. "It's probably Jessica letting off steam."

Lava is more like it, Billie thought.

The minister cleared his throat. "You're both students at SVU, is that right?"

Billie and Steven nodded.

Suddenly there was another crash and then the raised voices of Jessica and Mrs. Wakefield rang through the house.

"I told you it wouldn't work," Billie heard Jessica shout.

"It would have been fine," Mrs. Wakefield yelled back. "You took it out of the oven too soon."

Billie rolled her eyes and caught the distressed look on Steven's face. The soufflé must have fallen.

Steven leapt up and closed the door between the dining room and the kitchen, slightly muting the angry voices. "Sorry," he said. "Tempers are running a little high."

The minister dabbed at his forehead with a handkerchief and looked back down at his notes. "As I was saying," he continued, "Steven, you're in prelaw, and Billie, you're a musician?"

Billie beamed. Steven must have told Reverend Dexter about her guitar studies. He really was taking her music seriously! She was about to say something when the shouting started up again. Jessica and her mother had moved to the living room. Unfortunately there was no door to shut their angry voices out now.

"Nothing I do is right as far as you're concerned," Jessica snarled.

"If you'd do as I say, it wouldn't be a problem," Mrs. Wakefield yelled back, her voice becoming dangerously shrill.

"I don't want to do what you say. I want to do what I think is right," Jessica retorted.

Billie closed her eyes and tried to concentrate on what the minister was saying.

"I find it's preferable," the minister tried again, his frail voice rising, "for couples to write their own vows."

What? Write their own vows? With all the screaming from Jessica and Mrs. Wakefield, she mustn't have heard him right. "Can't we do the standard vows?" she asked. "You know, 'do you, Billie, take this man Steven . . .'" With everything else that was going on, the last thing she and Steven needed was to have to write their own vows.

"Yeah," Steven said. "I agree to have and to hold, and Billie agrees to cherish and obey . . ."

Wait a minute! "Obey?" Billie narrowed her dark blue eyes at Steven. She didn't like the sound of that.

Steven shrugged. "It's only a ceremony."

"I'm not marrying a dog trainer," Billie countered sharply.

The minister laughed and shook his head. "Now you see why I prefer that couples come up with their own vows." His eyes twinkled. "You two know what you want from marriage. That's what you should be pledging to each other."

Billie looked over at Reverend Dexter. Suddenly this slight, elderly man seemed incredibly wise. She and Steven knew what they wanted out of marriage. Writing their own vows would be a great chance to express it. How hard could it be?

Chapter Six

"Excuse me, Tom," Mrs. Wakefield said, bustling toward him in the backyard. "I need to get by."

"Sorry," Tom mumbled, jumping out of the way to avoid her crashing into him. Great. It was barely ten o'clock and already he was in the way. He shuffled over to where the caterers were setting up tables.

"Please, Tom," Isabella said, coming up behind him. Her arms were filled with strings of colored lights. "You're blocking the path. Why don't you stand over there?" She nodded vaguely in the direction of the pool.

Nice work, Watts, Tom thought. *Can you get in anyone else's way?*

Tom wandered over to where Winston and Danny were skimming leaves off the surface of the water.

"Can I help?" Tom asked.

Danny shook his head and leaned forward to

catch a branch from the corner. Tom stepped back at the same time that Winston stepped forward.

"Whoa!" Winston cried. His arms flailed as he teetered dangerously off balance by the edge of the pool. Tom's hand shot out and grabbed Winston's collar just in the nick of time.

"Hey," Winston complained. "I wasn't planning a morning swim. Why don't you go to the other end of the pool?"

Tom could feel his face burning a dark red. He was only trying to be helpful. He skulked over to the boxes of white tulips that the florist had delivered. Leaning over, he could smell their delicate aroma. He would give one to Elizabeth.

"Please," Alexandra snapped, grabbing it from him. She had come out of nowhere. "We're trying to arrange flowers here."

This was it! "Where would you like me to go?" he yelled to the busy yard.

Everyone looked up and pointed to the far end of the lawn. "Back there," they shouted in unison.

Tom groaned and started walking toward the end of the yard. *Fine.* He'd had enough of this. He was going to scale that back fence and be done with it.

Elizabeth came running out of the house as he got his first foothold.

"What are you doing?" she asked.

"I'm going over the wall," he said. "I know when I'm not wanted."

Elizabeth laughed and pulled at his green polo shirt. "Stop being silly. Mom has something for us to do."

106

"What?" Tom asked moodily. "Go play in traffic?"

Elizabeth crossed her tanned, graceful arms across her white tank top and tapped her foot in mock irritation. "Tom, you're being difficult."

Tom sighed. "Sorry, but everybody's been yelling at me and telling me I'm in the way. It's starting to get to me."

"Well, you can stop feeling useless now," Elizabeth teased. "We have a very important job to do. You and I are going to pick up my great-aunt Sylvia from the airport and bring her here for the out-of-town relatives' dinner. Afterward we'll drive her to her hotel."

"That doesn't sound too bad."

Elizabeth smiled. "I thought you'd like it." She stepped forward and put her warm bare arms around his neck. "Especially since we'll be out of the house."

Tom kissed the tip of her nose. "It does have that perk. And," he said, putting on his best silly Romeo accent, "it will be you and me, baby, all alone for the drive." He wrapped his strong arms around her, dipping her down like a ballroom dancer.

Elizabeth giggled. "There's one catch."

Tom sighed, pulling her back up. "What's that?"

"Nothing terrible." Elizabeth laughed. "Well, I've never actually met my aunt Sylvia. Even Mom hasn't seen her for over twenty years."

"Is that all?" Tom asked.

Elizabeth grimaced. "Mom says she's senile."

"Senile?" Tom asked. "As in a little forgetful?

Or as in completely out of it?" This was sounding more difficult by the minute.

"Her telegram said she would be arriving with Uncle Howard."

"Yeah?" Tom prompted.

Elizabeth winced slightly. "Uncle Howard has been . . . um, dead for a number of years."

Dead? Tom rolled his eyes. "Sounds like she'll fit in perfectly here at the madhouse."

Elizabeth's beautiful aquamarine eyes flashed impatiently. "If you'd rather stay here . . ."

"No, no, I'll go," Tom said, wrapping his arm around Elizabeth's shoulders and pulling her close. "It'll be my pleasure." He just loved dealing with senile old aunts.

They walked back toward the house and Tom opened the door for Elizabeth. The noise from within hit them like a tidal wave.

"When do we leave?" he pretended to shout, cupping his hands around his mouth.

Elizabeth hit him playfully. "It's not that bad. I can hear you if you speak up."

Tom grinned. The house *was* in a state of chaos, though. In the dining room Mrs. Wakefield was putting white doilies on the furniture while Jessica followed behind, picking them up just as quickly. In the living room Denise and Lila were moving the peach couch. First to the right and then to the left, depending on which Wakefield, Jessica or her mother, poked her head in and barked orders. Bruce was helping the caterers carry folding chairs through the hallways, and Mr. Wakefield was counting Perrier bottles in the kitchen.

"One thing, though," Tom shouted over the noise. "How are we going to recognize this mysterious Aunt Sylvia who no one has seen in twenty years?"

"Voilà," Elizabeth said, slipping a faded black-and-white photo out of the back pocket of her jean skirt. "Mom found this in one of the old family albums."

Tom looked closely at the picture. A man and a woman leaned against the wooden railing of a boardwalk, a beach in the background. Their arms were loosely wrapped around each other. The woman's hair was teased back and bleached blond. She wore a pair of ruby-studded, cat-eye sunglasses and a halter dress with a giant flowered pattern. The man had a crewcut. The sleeves of his white T-shirt were rolled almost to his shoulders. In the white border around the photo was the year 1956.

"This is forty years old!" Tom exclaimed.

"Remarkable, isn't it?"

"Yeah," Tom agreed. "But how are we going to recognize her? Forty years ago she was a middle-aged woman—now she must be pushing eighty."

Elizabeth shrugged. "How many little old ladies can there be getting off the plane from Phoenix?"

"I hear it's a big retirement city," Tom said. He could imagine a hundred little old ladies pouring off the plane from Phoenix.

"Maybe," Elizabeth countered. "But she's coming for Steven's wedding. She'll be looking for us, too."

"If she remembers why she got on the plane in the first place." Now every one of those hundred little old ladies in Tom's head was wondering what she was doing in Sweet Valley, California, anyway.

Elizabeth smiled. "Details, details. It gets us out of the house, right?"

"Right," Tom agreed. "Maybe we'll take another romantic ride along the coastline."

"And leave poor Aunt Sylvia wandering around the airport alone?" Elizabeth asked with mock seriousness.

"Never," Tom said. "Perish the thought."

"Elizabeth, honey," Mrs. Wakefield called, her heels crunching along the gravel driveway.

Elizabeth turned, her keys dangling in her hand. "What is it, Mom?" She hoped there wasn't some last-minute task to do here at the house. Tom was already in the Jeep.

"I wanted to tell you what a help you've been," Mrs. Wakefield said, slightly out of breath. She reached forward and gave Elizabeth a big hug.

"Oh, Mom, you don't have to thank me. I'm doing what any daughter would do."

"No," Mrs. Wakefield said. "It's more than that. I don't know what I'd do without you. Jessica is being impossible."

Elizabeth grimaced. She hoped her mother wasn't about to go on an anti-Jessica rant. After listening to Jessica's complaining on the drive down, she wasn't in the mood for any more sniping. She shifted her weight to her other foot and looked guiltily toward the Jeep. Tom was probably afraid the trip to the airport was being called off.

"But I don't mean this to turn into a Jessica gripe," Mrs. Wakefield said. "I'm sure you've heard enough from her."

"Well, you know Jessica."

"Yes." Her mother sighed. "Sometimes I wonder if she really is my daughter. She can be so bossy and stubborn."

Elizabeth stifled a laugh. What more evidence did her mother need?

"But then," Mrs. Wakefield went on, "I know you're my daughter. If she's your twin, she must be my daughter too."

Elizabeth laughed. "She means well, Mom."

"I know," Mrs. Wakefield said. "But I wish she could be more like you at times like this. Sensible and dependable."

"Thanks, Mom," Elizabeth said. "Maybe if you'd let Jess make a few decisions or even divide up some tasks, things wouldn't be so bad."

But Elizabeth could see her mother wasn't listening.

"Be careful," Mrs. Wakefield cried as Bruce and Winston wrestled an enormous ficus tree toward the front door. "You have to tilt it." She watched for a moment more until they'd successfully navigated the entrance. "Honestly," she said, turning back to Elizabeth. "I've got to watch every little detail. Were you saying something, Liz?"

Elizabeth shrugged. "Nothing important."

Mrs. Wakefield smiled. "I know I can trust you implicitly. You'd never bungle anything. I don't know what I'd do without you."

111

"You're going to make my head swell if you don't cut it out," Elizabeth joked.

"I'm serious," Mrs. Wakefield said. "When I ask you to do something, I know I can rest easy and it will all come out right. I don't have to give it another thought. It's such a comfort."

Elizabeth smiled. "I should leave, Mom. I don't want to be late to meet Aunt Sylvia's plane."

Mrs. Wakefield nodded. "I gave you that picture, right?"

"Yes, Mom," Elizabeth said. "Both Tom and I have studied it closely."

"It's not up-to-date."

"We've mentally added forty years."

"Of course," Mrs. Wakefield said, hugging her once more. "Why am I questioning you? I know you can handle it."

Elizabeth patted her mother's back. "Calm down, Mom—everything will be fine."

Mrs. Wakefield laughed. "I just hate to see you go. You're the only one I can really depend on. Who knows what's going to fall apart next?"

"Well, you can count on Tom and me, Mom," Elizabeth said, walking toward the Jeep. "So that's one less thing to worry about."

Jessica sat, her bare legs tucked under her on a red-and-black-plaid blanket, looking around the most beautiful meadow she'd ever seen, and smiled. The lush green grass was dotted with violet wildflowers. In the distance she could see the thick, dark woods and a pond where she imagined deer came to drink. But best of all, it was Mike who had brought her here. Along with a picnic lunch and a portable radio that was softly playing Billie Holiday.

Mike hadn't told her where they were going on their date, so she'd chosen to wear her new honey-colored sundress with a matching headband to pull back her long blond hair, and a pair of open-toed high heels. Her shoes lay discarded at the end of the blanket. Not the best choice for the outdoors, but her outfit did show off her deep golden tan.

This is the best date ever, she thought. In truth, she'd been a little nervous about going out with Mike again, even if they had agreed to go slow. But an afternoon date was innocent, right?

"How did you ever find this place?" Jessica asked dreamily. "It's like a piece of heaven."

Mike rolled onto his side and looked up at her, his hazel eyes twinkling a golden green in the sunlight. "I'm glad you like it," he said. "I hope it's not too rustic for you."

"Not at all. Once I took off my heels, it wasn't so bad."

Mike laughed. "I should have told you to wear a T-shirt, jeans, and hiking boots, like me."

"But then I wouldn't be getting any sun on my legs," Jessica said. She leaned back on her elbows, stretching out her long, slender legs. She shivered a little as a cool breeze rippled across the thin summer dress.

"Are you cold?" Mike asked. She liked the sound of his deep, gruff voice.

Jessica shrugged. "A little. My legs *are* bare."

"I know," Mike said softly.

Jessica stared at the handsome, desirable face of her ex-husband. With his tousled dark hair and sensuous lips, he was better looking than any rock star. A shiver of excitement ran down her spine like an electric charge. They were so close. All she had to do was lean forward and she'd tumble into his arms. *I've got to behave,* she thought, sitting up.

"So, how *did* you find this place?" she asked again.

Mike turned and looked off into the distance. "My uncle used to take me here when I was a kid," he said. "We used to fish that pond." He pointed to the water in the distance.

"I can't imagine you fishing," Jessica said. The truth was, she had a very difficult time imagining Mike as a little kid, period.

"I never caught much," Mike said. "But it was good to be here with my uncle." He looked at her. "Though not as good as it is being here with you."

Jessica took a deep breath. Her senses were clouding. This close, she could smell the faint scent of leather coming from him. It reminded her of a night, a long time ago, when they'd slept under the stars with only his jacket to keep them warm. Their wedding night. She felt a deep stirring in her heart.

"Maybe we'd better go," Mike said, sitting up abruptly.

"But we just got here," Jessica said. "What's the matter?"

He looked down at her, his eyes smoldering. Obviously the windblown natural look she'd gone for on their date was having an effect. *That's the problem,* she thought. *He's as attracted to me as I am to him.*

She drew her knees up to her chest. "Let's eat," she said with a half smile. "That will take our minds off things."

Mike groaned and flopped back down beside her. "Maybe we shouldn't face each other while we do it."

"Are my manners that terrible?" Jessica teased.

"Don't, Jess," Mike said hoarsely. "If we're going to start over again, you can't be flirting with me like that."

"Okay," Jessica said. Mike was right. If they were going to start from the beginning, then they'd better stop acting as if they'd once been lovers.

"As a matter of fact," Mike said, "I think we should try to forget about our history. For the next few days let's pretend we have no past. We're two people who are getting to know each other."

"Deal," Jessica said. "So can we eat facing each other now?"

Mike laughed.

She reached into the picnic basket and pulled out a large hero sandwich. Opening it up, she saw it consisted of salami, cheese that smelled like old socks, and a liberal dose of raw onions.

"Yuck," Jessica gasped. "This should certainly cool us off. After eating this we won't be able to get within ten feet of each other."

Mike grinned. "A safety measure," he said. "But with your luscious looks, I'm afraid even that won't help."

Jessica smiled and fought the urge to reach out

for him. *We have a deal,* she reminded herself, and went for the mineral water instead. *This is a proper, innocent date.* Inside the picnic basket her hand felt something cold and slimy.

"Pickles?" she said incredulously.

"Second line of defense." Mike chuckled. "Eat up. Those were marinated in garlic. They're guaranteed to kill our breath."

"If they don't kill us first," Jessica said with a laugh.

"I can't believe we're going to be late," Elizabeth mumbled to herself, fumbling with her seat belt. Now she couldn't even get out of the Jeep.

Tom reached across and unsnapped it for her. "Calm down. We'll get there."

They started across the parking lot toward the entrance of the airport. Tom's long, quick strides in his black athletic sneakers made her run to keep up, her loose blond hair streaming behind her.

"And I thought I was fast on my feet," Elizabeth said, panting, as the terminal doors opened with a swoosh. "It's a good thing I wore my tennis shoes, or you would have left me in the dust." She pulled back her hair and clipped it with a tortoiseshell clasp.

Tom grinned. "I wasn't a football star just because of my good looks." He crouched down, faking left and then right. Suddenly he sprinted forward.

Elizabeth laughed as a couple of tourists gaped at him. "Tom," she scolded him. "You're scaring people."

He draped an arm around Elizabeth. "There's Information," he said, pointing up ahead.

Elizabeth looked up at the blinking mechanical board and scanned the Arrivals column. Phoenix Flight 602 had already landed.

"Oh no," Elizabeth gasped. "It was early."

"Don't worry," Tom said. "She's old. How far can she get? She's probably still walking down the ramp."

"We'd better hurry," Elizabeth said, starting to run.

A couple of tourists jumped out of their way.

"Now who's scaring people?" Tom said, running close behind.

Elizabeth's heart fell as they approached Aunt Sylvia's gate. The entire area was deserted. Even the flight crew had gone.

Elizabeth looked around helplessly. No Aunt Sylvia. "Now what are we going to do?"

"Luggage," Tom said, and started to sprint away.

"Luggage, right," Elizabeth murmured. Aunt Sylvia would have a bag. Probably too big and heavy for an old lady to carry. They'd find her sitting at the luggage carousel, forlornly watching her suitcase go around and around on the conveyor belt.

Elizabeth followed closely behind Tom as they wound their way through the crowd. By the time they got to the baggage area, most of the suitcases were gone. But a few elderly ladies were milling around.

Elizabeth rushed up to the nearest one. "Aunt Sylvia?" she called.

The woman turned and looked at her blankly through thick bifocals.

"Sorry," Elizabeth mumbled, and started toward another gray head. She stopped as this woman was quickly surrounded by a large family of relatives.

Elizabeth spied one more frail figure, bent over a large brown suitcase. "Aunt Sylvia," she cried.

The woman ignored her.

Elizabeth ran toward her and touched her arm.

The elderly lady looked up, her faded blue eyes wide with alarm.

Elizabeth dropped her hand. "Sorry, I thought you were my aunt Sylvia."

The woman shook her head.

Tom came up behind Elizabeth. "No luck. I met a Myrtle, an Eleanor, and two Alices. Not one of those ladies is Aunt Sylvia."

"Where could she be?" Elizabeth asked, trying to keep the desperation out of her voice. They had to find her!

Tom's eyes darted back and forth. "The airline desk. We'll check and make sure she was on the plane."

"Good idea," Elizabeth said. "She could have missed it."

They crossed the hall and went to the airline desk. "Did you have a passenger named Sylvia Johnson on your list for Flight 602?" Elizabeth asked.

A steward in a dark blue jacket gave them the official version of a smile. Elizabeth watched as his fingers flew over the computer keyboard. "Mrs. Johnson, S.," he said. "Seat 3B, nonsmoking, dietetic meal." He ran his finger along the screen. "Checked in and accounted for."

Elizabeth groaned. Now what?

Tom stepped forward. "And there's no way she could have missed the flight?"

The steward shook his head. "Absolutely not. She arrived here promptly at two fifteen P.M. with all the other passengers."

Elizabeth stepped back from the counter and wrapped her arms around herself. Suddenly, in her thin white tank top, she was feeling very cold.

Tom came over and gave her a hug. "She couldn't have gotten far. We'll page her."

"Good idea," Elizabeth said, brightening. "Information can do that."

They headed toward the front of the terminal.

Elizabeth hesitated as they passed a group of elderly women sipping tea in one of the airport cafeterias. A newspaper with the logo *The Arizona Times* caught her eye. "You go ahead, Tom. I want to talk to these ladies."

Tom nodded and kept going.

Elizabeth walked up to the women. "Hi, I'm Elizabeth Wakefield. I'm looking for my aunt. Her name is Sylvia Johnson. Do you know her?"

One of the ladies with a blue tint to her coiffured hair tittered. "We may be old, young lady, and know a lot of people. But we haven't been around long enough to know everyone in the world."

The other three started to laugh too.

Elizabeth felt her face blush deeply. "I didn't mean that," she stuttered, feeling close to tears. "I noticed your newspaper. My aunt Sylvia got off the plane from Phoenix. I hoped maybe she'd been on the same flight as you."

119

The women shook their heads.

The blue-haired lady motioned to the seat next to her at the table. "Sit down, dear, and tell us what happened."

Elizabeth slipped onto the wooden chair "My boyfriend and I were late," she said miserably. "Now I can't find my aunt Sylvia anywhere."

The elderly lady sitting across from Elizabeth took her hand and patted it gently. "Have you tried the car-rental agencies? Maybe she got tired of waiting."

Elizabeth jumped to her feet. "Of course!" Aunt Sylvia must have given up on them and was going to drive herself to Sweet Valley. "Thank you so much." Elizabeth rushed off toward the car-rental agencies.

The woman at the first rental counter shook her head. At the second counter the man shrugged. Next up was the Americar counter. Suddenly, though, through the plate-glass window, Elizabeth's attention was drawn to an elderly man wearing a gray cap. He was stepping into a beige Americar rental. In the passenger seat was an elderly woman in a pair of ruby-studded, cat-eye sunglasses. She hadn't seen the man's face, but Elizabeth didn't need the photo in her pocket to tell her who the woman was. In those glasses, she would have known her aunt Sylvia anywhere!

The car began pulling away. "Wait! Stop!" Elizabeth cried, running through the double doors and waving her arms. But neither old person turned. The car sped off. They were getting away!

"What is it?" Tom asked, running up to her as

120

the announcement for Aunt Sylvia started to resound through the airport. "I heard you screaming."

Elizabeth turned to Tom, her whole body trembling. "That was Aunt Sylvia," she wailed. "She's been abducted!"

Chapter Seven

Jessica and Mike walked hand in hand up the front path of her parents' house. *What a perfect day,* Jessica thought. *First the picnic and then a scary double feature. I almost hate for it to end.* She hadn't really believed that she and Mike could go out and have a good time together. But they had. And they'd stuck to their deal, too. Mike hadn't even held her hand until they'd pulled up at the house.

They reached the front stoop, and Mike turned toward her. *I hope we don't have to stick to that deal now,* Jessica thought. Even a "first date" could end with a kiss.

Mike raised his eyebrows and spoke in a mock Transylvanian accent. "Doo note be afred tonight," he said, baring his teeth.

Jessica giggled. The vampire double feature they had just watched had been more laughs than chills. Still, she had to admit she'd been pretty scared once or twice.

"I'll wear a cross and hang garlic all over my room," she teased.

"Old wives' tales," Mike said. "Worthless against your modern-day vampire."

Jessica felt a shiver go up her spine. She remembered how a handsome vampire in one of the movies had torn the cross from his victim's neck before sinking his teeth into her. The girl hadn't seemed to mind, though. She'd almost welcomed it. Jessica shuddered.

Mike put his arm around her and laughed. "It was only a movie."

Jessica lowered her eyes. Mike's arm around her was sending shivers of a different kind up her spine now. "Why do the bad guys always have to be so handsome?"

Mike smiled. "I don't know. I guess we're lucky that way."

"You weren't bad at all today," Jessica said faintly.

Mike cupped her chin, gently tilting her face toward him. "Maybe I should make up for lost time." His golden eyes smoldered with desire.

Jessica closed her own yearning eyes and softly parted her lips in anticipation of his kiss. She could feel Mike's warm breath on her cheek, moving closer. Closer. Three, two, one . . .

The front door flew open. "Jessica's home!" the shrill voices of her aunts Eloise, Matilda, and Agnes screamed in unison.

Jessica's eyes snapped wide open. Mike jumped back. *Talk about bad timing,* she thought.

Her aunts surrounded her, practically pushing

Mike off the stoop. They poked and prodded and gushed.

"Look how big she's gotten."

"What a nice figure."

"Who was that boy? I hope we didn't frighten him away."

Jessica groaned as she watched Mike hightail it back to his motorcycle. So much for him being fearless. Who could blame him, though? A stampede of wild elephants couldn't have made more noise.

With an aunt pulling on each arm and another pushing from behind, Jessica soon found herself in the middle of the living room. Her uncles joined in and the bear hugs began. By the end of it she felt as if all her ribs had been broken. Her cheeks were swollen from being pinched.

"Next time *I'm* checking into a hotel," Jessica mumbled.

Jessica was beginning to pick up warning signs that a second round of squeezing was about to begin when the phone rang.

"I'll get it," she cried, extracting herself from Aunt Agnes's powerful grip. It was like wrestling with a sumo champion.

Mrs. Wakefield beat her to the phone, but Jessica dived behind her to hide. *Please,* she thought. *Let it be Elizabeth on her way home.* She needed someone to share this abuse.

"Oh, hello, Aunt Sylvia," Mrs. Wakefield clucked. "How are you? How is your hotel?"

Jessica rolled her eyes. "Not another relative," she grumbled. How would she survive? "I'd take a vampire's bite over a roomful of relatives any day!"

*   *   *

"The hotel's fine, Alice," Tom said into the pay phone to Mrs. Wakefield, his voice high-pitched and creaky. "I'm settled in nicely."

He and Elizabeth were standing in the elegant lobby of what should have been Aunt Sylvia's hotel. Gilded framed mirrors lined the long walls. A large chandelier hung suspended from the high ornate ceiling, its crystals glinting in the soft light of the table lamps that flanked the lobby's blue velvet sofas.

Elizabeth pulled on his arm.

"What, Liz?" he asked, covering the mouthpiece.

"Tell Mom Aunt Sylvia's too tired to come over for the out-of-town relatives' dinner."

Tom got back on the phone. "Aunt Sylvia is—er, I mean," he raised his voice three octaves. "Oh, my. With these sweet young ones calling me Aunt Sylvia all day, I forgot and nearly started doing it myself." Tom gripped the phone tightly, his face burning a flustered red.

"Do you have a cold?" Mrs. Wakefield asked through the phone. "You sound hoarse."

"No, no," Tom said, raising his voice to an even higher pitch. "I'm a bit tired. I'll have to miss tonight's dinner to rest up. I'm sorry."

"Yes, of course, Aunt Sylvia," Mrs. Wakefield said. "Don't worry about that. We'll see you tomorrow."

"Okay," Tom said, his voice beginning to hurt from the strain. "I'm sending Elizabeth and her young man home now. They've been

126

absolute angels. Bye-bye." Tom hung up the phone and sighed.

Under other circumstances pretending to be an eighty-year-old woman might have seemed funny. *But it doesn't now,* he thought. If Mrs. Wakefield ever figured out how he'd fooled her, he'd be in the doghouse for the rest of his life.

He turned to Elizabeth. "This is crazy, Liz. How long am I supposed to go on impersonating your aunt Sylvia?"

"Until we find her," Elizabeth answered grimly. "I can't let my mother down. She's counting on me. What would she think if she found out we'd lost Aunt Sylvia? Or worse, that she'd been abducted right from under our noses?"

"You're jumping to conclusions, Liz," Tom said. "We don't know what happened yet. She could have gotten tired of waiting and some nice old man gave her a lift." He was trying to sound hopeful, but he was as worried as Elizabeth.

"Then why isn't she here?" Elizabeth moaned.

They had already asked at the long, polished desk, where the concierge stood in a crisp navy blue uniform. The hotel had Aunt Sylvia's reservation, but there had been no sign of her.

I don't know, Tom thought, scanning the lobby again. He stared into the mirrors, letting them reflect his line of vision around the room. Maybe he would catch sight of Aunt Sylvia around a corner or hidden behind one of the potted plants. But no luck. She wasn't there. He looked over at Elizabeth and saw she was chewing her lower lip. She only did that when she was really nervous.

"I'm sure it's nothing sinister," Tom said confidently. "She probably forgot where she was supposed to be and checked into the wrong hotel."

"You really think so, Tom?" Elizabeth asked, her eyes pleading for reassurance. "We'll find her tomorrow, right?"

"Sure," Tom said encouragingly. "How far can she get? Remember, we're two young supersleuths and she's only one old lady." *Who up to now has managed to completely elude us,* he thought bleakly. But he certainly wasn't going to mention that.

"I guess you're right," Elizabeth said wearily. "Well, we'd better get back to my house. We don't want my mother getting suspicious."

As they walked out to the Jeep, Tom put his arm around her. "It'll be okay," he whispered. "I promise."

Neither of them said much during the car ride home. But Tom couldn't ignore Elizabeth's tense, pursed lips as she navigated the freeway. More than anything he wished he could do something to ease her worry. But it would have to wait until tomorrow.

Elizabeth's relatives greeted them at the door like a hurricane. For the next half hour Tom hardly saw Elizabeth as she was passed from one overly enthusiastic relative to the next.

"I'm black-and-blue," she gasped when she finally broke free.

Tom chuckled. He'd had his hand politely shaken and had then been relegated to the side of the living room. He'd never been so happy to be an outsider before.

"Thank goodness dinner is starting," Elizabeth said, wobbling to her chair. "I'm going to collapse into this seat before they descend upon me again."

Tom sat down next to her at the dining-room table and patted her hand. "I hope the food will revive you."

"Fat chance," Jessica said, slipping into the chair across from them. "Maybe a hospital stay. I need an X ray. I'm sure they've broken my ribs."

"Ow," Elizabeth said, shaking, "don't make me laugh. It hurts."

Jessica snorted. "Did all this damage come from these pythons or did Aunt Sylvia give you a working over too?"

"Speaking of Sylvia," Aunt Matilda called from the end of the table. "How is she?"

Tom looked at Elizabeth and she looked at him. Their eyes widened.

"Fine," they shouted in unison.

"What's she been up to?" Uncle Clifford asked.

"Elizabeth?" Tom prompted. But Elizabeth had conveniently filled her mouth with food and nodded for him to go on.

"Well," Tom said, trying not to panic. "She's . . ." What did old ladies do? "Bingo," he cried. "She plays a lot of bingo. A big winner, right, Liz?"

Elizabeth nodded furiously and shoved some more food in her mouth.

"And church socials," Tom said. "Lots of church socials. She's big on collecting for charities."

"Really?" Aunt Agnes said. "I always thought Aunt Sylvia was rather tightfisted."

"No, no." Tom shook his head vigorously.

"Since she's started winning in bingo, she's become very generous."

"That's funny," Uncle Willie said. "She always used to complain about her bad luck."

"Not since she got her lucky charm," Tom improvised.

"Very special charm," Elizabeth croaked, giving him a warning look.

What was Elizabeth worried about? He was handling this fine. "One night she won over a hundred dollars," Tom said. Actually, he was beginning to enjoy himself.

Elizabeth kicked him under the table.

"I mean all together," he gulped, "over her entire bingo career. It was when she played the slot machines that she—"

Elizabeth kicked him even harder.

"Hmm," Uncle Randolph mused. "Maybe I can talk her into a trip to Vegas. I could use that kind of luck. Hey, Eloise, did I ever tell you about the time I went to Vegas . . ."

Tom let out a deep sigh of relief as the conversation turned away from Aunt Sylvia. One more kick from Elizabeth and *he* might end up in the hospital himself.

It was early morning when Bruce stepped out of his attorney's office into the long, carpeted hallway of Ballard, Smythe, Loeb & Hobbs, the most prestigious law firm in Sweet Valley.

He gave his lawyer, Daniel Loeb, a tentative handshake, glad to be outside his musty office. Except for the formidable oak desk and the two high-backed client chairs, every square foot in there had been dominated by imposing bookcases, crowded with dusty law tomes that towered above him accusingly. *How could you go behind Lila's back!* they seemed to shout.

Bruce cleared his throat and brushed a crease out of his tan khakis. "So you don't think I'm taking an unnecessary step at this time?"

"Not at all," Mr. Loeb said, removing his glasses and wiping them carefully. "With a bank balance like yours, you have a lot to protect. There's nothing wrong with using a little foresight. A pre-engagement prenuptial agreement is a fine idea." He replaced his glasses on the end of his sharply tipped nose.

"Even though we don't have any wedding plans on the horizon?" Bruce asked. The more he talked about it, the more doubtful he became. After all, he and Lila weren't even engaged.

"Doesn't matter," Mr. Loeb said. "It sends the right signals. Gold diggers beware."

"Lila's not a gold digger," Bruce said. Far from it. "She has plenty of her own money."

"Then why is she after yours?" Mr. Loeb asked.

"Lila isn't after my money," Bruce said. *Right?* he thought. But wasn't it Lila who was always saying, "You can never be too thin or too rich"?

"Of course not," Mr. Loeb said, a flicker of amusement playing across his face. "But it's funny what divorce will do to people, even people who seem completely virtuous and unselfish."

Bruce raised an eyebrow. *Virtuous* and *unselfish* were not words he would use to describe Lila. But did that mean she would try to get all his money?

He shook away the image of Mr. Fowler gasping for breath in Lila's choke hold. "We're not going to get divorced," Bruce said firmly.

Again that smug look as Mr. Loeb flicked his tongue across his lips. "Then neither of you should mind the existence of this type of contract."

"No, I guess not," Bruce said. But he was really glad Lila didn't know he was here. There was something sneaky about the whole thing.

Bruce shook hands with his lawyer once more and then turned to go, smacking right into another client of the firm.

"Excuse me," he said, turning to see if there was any damage.

There was plenty! Lila stood before him, her feet planted apart. She was wearing a smart-looking gray pantsuit. And like her outfit, the look on her face was all business. Her dark brown eyes glared back at him.

"So," she charged indignantly, "this is what you've been up to."

"What are you doing here?" he croaked. But he needn't have bothered. It was obvious. Ms. Taylor-Hobbs, the other matrimonial partner of the law firm, was standing right beside her.

Lila's eyes narrowed to small, blazing slits. "I asked you first," she hissed, tossing back her thick chestnut hair. "I suppose this is one of your mysterious errands?"

"Oh, and I guess you have an early morning dentist appointment somewhere in the building," Bruce shot back, his voice rising.

"I can't believe you're doing this to me,"

Lila snarled. "How can I ever trust you?"

"Me?" Bruce shouted, throwing up his arms. "Look who's talking. It's obvious I can't trust you." Maybe coming to see his lawyer hadn't been such a bad idea after all.

"Bruce, Lila," the lawyers cried in unison. "Let's calm down a minute."

Bruce's breath was coming in ragged gasps. To think he'd been worried about her, feeling guilty about going behind her back. And here all along she'd been next door!

Ms. Taylor-Hobbs stepped between them. "It's good you're both here. It shows you really want to make this work. Why don't you two go down to the conference room at the end of the hall and talk it out?"

Bruce gave Mr. Loeb a questioning look. He wasn't going to do anything Lila's lawyer said unless his own lawyer gave him the go-ahead.

Mr. Loeb nodded. "Ms. Taylor-Hobbs has made a very good suggestion. I'm sure that after a few minutes of quiet talk, you'll get this little problem hammered out."

That's what I'm worried about, Bruce thought. *Two of us go in and after a little hammering only one of us comes out.* He looked over at Lila. The deadly sparks in her eyes seemed to have softened.

"What do you think?" he asked her cautiously. If she was willing, he was too.

"I guess so." She sniffed. "If you think it will do any good."

"If it doesn't work, we can always duke it out on the playground," he said, half jokingly.

133

"You're bigger than me," Lila said coyly.

"I'll let you have the first shot," Bruce said, and gave her a smile.

Lila's eyes brightened and she clenched her fist.

"I said only if it doesn't work out." Bruce laughed, taking a step back.

"Doesn't give me much incentive. Does it?" Lila asked, grinning.

"Come on, you," Bruce said, throwing his arm around her shoulders. "Don't be such a trouble-maker."

"Me," Lila said. "You're the one . . ."

But he silenced her with a kiss and safely walked her to the conference room.

Elizabeth stifled a long yawn as she joined the line at the car-rental agency. She and Tom had been on the road early that morning, heading back to the airport. She'd realized last night that the first step in finding Aunt Sylvia was to find the old man who had rented the getaway car.

"Why do these brilliant thoughts always come to me in the middle of the night?" She sighed to herself. She hadn't had a wink of sleep after that. Her reflection in the airport's huge windows showed that. She tucked in a loose corner of her pale pink T-shirt and straightened the seam in her long flowered skirt.

"Were you saying something, Liz?" Tom asked, joining her on the line. He looked wide awake in his bright red polo shirt and freshly pressed khakis. He handed her a Styrofoam cup full of steaming black coffee.

Elizabeth shook her head, her blond ponytail moving back and forth. "Don't mind me. I'm only muttering."

"Well, drink up," Tom said, taking a sip of his coffee. "I don't want you falling asleep on the job."

Elizabeth took a big gulp and felt her head slowly beginning to clear. "Hey, I came up with this idea when I was half asleep."

"And it was a good thing you did," Tom said. "Now let's hope you took down that license-plate number correctly."

"Don't worry about that," Elizabeth said. After the fright she'd had, seeing Aunt Sylvia driven off like that, the number was practically engraved in her mind. "I wish I'd gotten a better look at that old man." All she'd seen was his gray cap.

"With any luck," Tom said, "we'll be able to find out where he's headed."

"Do you really think a kidnapper would advertise where he's going?" Elizabeth asked. If she were a criminal, that was the last thing she'd do.

"Remember, he doesn't know we're after him," Tom said.

That's the one thing in our favor, Elizabeth thought. *Now if we can just find out who he is.*

"Next," the woman called at the Americar counter. She wore the official green-and-blue-striped uniform with a nameplate saying PAT JEFFREYS, CUSTOMER SERVICE REPRESENTATIVE, pinned above her chest.

Elizabeth stepped up to the counter. "I need some information about one of your cars. We were late picking up my aunt yesterday and I saw her driving off with a strange man. I have the license-plate

135

number, but I need the man's name and address."

"I'm sorry," the woman said politely. "Company policy prohibits me from sharing any information with you regarding our other customers. If you'd like to rent a car, I'd be happy to help you."

Elizabeth's mouth dropped. "But this is an emergency."

The woman shrugged. "I don't make up the rules."

"Come on, Liz," Tom said, taking her arm.

"Wait," Elizabeth said, standing firm. She had to get that information. Who knew what kind of monster had Aunt Sylvia in his clutches? She leaned over the counter. "Please, you don't understand. We don't know how else to find her."

The woman shook her head slowly. "I'm sorry." She indicated the long line. "There are other customers waiting."

"Ms. Jeffreys," Elizabeth tried again, frustrated tears rising in her eyes. "An old lady's life might be at risk. You've got to help us."

The woman hesitated for a second, glancing back and forth. "I never did believe in all these rules and regulations," she said in a much friendlier tone. "What's the license number?"

Elizabeth sighed deeply. "Thank you." She passed over the piece of paper with the number jotted on it. "It was a beige four-door, if that helps."

The woman punched up her computer screen and scanned the entries. "You're right. A beige four-door with this license number was rented by a Mr. Carl Lister from Anchorage, Alaska."

"Does that name ring a bell, Liz?" Tom asked.

Elizabeth frowned. *Lister. Carl Lister,* she thought.

No. I'm sure I've never heard that name before. She shook her head. "Does it say where he was heading?"

The woman flicked through several pages on her screen. "You're in luck. He's scheduled to return the car today in Santa Carmine."

"I know where that is," Elizabeth said excitedly. "It's a beach town about three hours away."

"Two and a half," the woman said, "if you take the coast road. But he's supposed to return the car by noon."

"Oh no." Elizabeth groaned. That didn't leave them much time.

"Give me a second," the woman said. "I'll get you our map. It shows the quickest routes between our outlets."

Elizabeth waited, feeling the adrenaline pump through her body. "What do you think, Tom?" she asked. "Can we make it?"

"It'll be a close call," he said.

"But if we hurry," Elizabeth said, "we can catch him there and find out what he's done with Aunt Sylvia. Maybe she'll even be in the car with him."

The woman came back with the map and spread it on the counter. Boxes advertising the rental locations showed every few inches.

"Here's our Santa Carmine branch," she said, pointing to one of the boxes. She glanced at her watch. "If you start now, you might make it before twelve."

"Thank you," Elizabeth said. "Thank you very, very much." She grabbed the map and they ran for the door, her thoughts already flying down the highway.

     *   *   *

Steven leaned back in the brown leather armchair in his father's den. Before him on the mahogany desk lay a blank piece of paper. Who was he trying to kid? He couldn't write his own wedding vows. He didn't even know where to begin.

He chewed on the end of his pen. "C'mon, Wakefield," he said to himself. "You've done harder stuff than this. Remember that sociology paper last semester? You didn't even know what you were talking about then." Maybe he didn't know what he was talking about now, either.

Steven tapped his pen on the top of the desk. What was marriage, anyway? And what exactly was he supposed to be vowing to do? "Maybe I should have paid more attention in philosophy class," he said with a sigh.

He drummed his fingers on the wooden arm of the chair, but his mind wouldn't budge. *This is crazy,* he thought. *I'm getting nowhere fast.* Maybe he just needed a break. He reached for the newspaper. First he'd relax and read the sports section. Then he'd get back to those vows.

As he thumbed through the paper, a headline caught his eye. STUDY: 50% OF MARRIAGES END IN DIVORCE, he read. Stephen gasped. *They must be kidding,* he thought. One out of every two marriages fails? How could that be? Why were people even bothering?

"If I had a fifty percent chance of being struck by lightning whenever I went out," he said to himself, "I'd never leave the house." Was he crazy to sign up for such a chancy thing?

Steven quickly scanned the rest of the article. Not much meat to it, just statistics. But it sounded pretty gloomy. "Still," he said, "the other fifty percent manage to stay married." They must be doing something right. *But what?*

Steven grabbed his car keys and headed for the door. There was one way to find out. He gunned his engine and headed toward town. In his experience everything that worked eventually found its way into a book. Sweet Valley's biggest bookstore had a section devoted to self-help. He was sure he could find something there on what made relationships work.

Steven parked his car at the bottom of Main Street, a road dotted with clothing boutiques, antique stores, and fancy cafés. He rushed toward the bookstore, weaving his way through the busy sidewalk filled with morning shoppers.

Once inside he followed the color-coded signs to the self-help section. It took up almost a whole aisle. Steven walked from one end of it to the other, scanning the titles. He'd never realized people had so many problems. Anger, envy, gambling, intimacy, relationships. Now he was getting somewhere. Relationships. "There must be stuff on marriage here," he murmured.

He pulled down every book that had *marriage* in the title.

"Excuse me." A middle-aged lady in a canary yellow jogging suit approached him. "Can you tell me where I can find a book on astrology?"

"Sorry," Steven said. "I don't work here."

"Oh," she said, looking perplexed. "I thought you were stocking the shelves."

Steven followed her gaze down to his feet. He'd created a stack of books up to the knees of his jeans. "Just shopping like you," he said. He scooped the first five books off the top of the pile and ran to the register. *With all this stuff to read, I'd better get cracking,* he thought.

Leaving the bookstore, he turned left and walked up the leafy street to the Sweet Valley town library. He found a quiet corner and opened the first book. He needed to give this stuff his undivided attention. *After all,* he reasoned, *my marriage is at stake.*

Lila looked up as the large grandfather clock in the corner chimed eleven. Another half hour had slipped away in the conference room of the law offices of Ballard, Smythe, Loeb & Hobbs.

"Bruce," she said, snuggling deeper into his arms. "We've been in here so long, our lawyers probably think we're going to come out with a fifty-page contract."

"Have we?" Bruce murmured, his eyes closed. "It doesn't feel that long to me."

Lila smiled and traced his full, smooth lips with her finger and then leaned forward for another kiss. Bruce was right. Once they started kissing, time stood still. But glancing at the clock, she knew it had been over an hour since the lawyers had escorted them in here to iron things out.

Lila giggled at the memory. After the first five minutes of posturing, she'd ended up in Bruce's lap in a long, luxurious kiss. It was always like that with Bruce. She could start out raging at him. Even thinking of him as her worst enemy. But somehow, as soon as they were alone, she ended up in his arms.

"What is it about you, Bruce Patman?" she whispered. "You've put a spell on me. We're supposed to be working on this agreement and all I want to do is kiss you."

"Well, it must be the same one you put on me," Bruce said. "Because I turn to putty in your hands."

Lila sighed, her lips once again seeking out Bruce's. The clock chimed, and she reluctantly came up for air. She smoothed down her paisley blouse. "How about if we agree to stop working on an agreement? No more fighting between us."

"But making up is so much fun," Bruce whispered. He ran his fingers through her soft brown hair.

Lila could feel the sparks shooting through her body. She shivered a little as he pushed her hair to one side, exposing the back of her pale, slender neck. "We can have the making up without the fights."

"Okay," Bruce murmured, planting a series of kisses along her neck. "How about we leave the lawyers to work out the negotiations?"

Fine, Lila thought, sighing contentedly. "Then we can meet with them after they've worked out all the details. Let them do the dirty work."

"See, we can agree," Bruce said. "We came up with a great idea. Hey, maybe *we* should be lawyers. We could start our own firm."

"Not a chance," Lila said, sitting up. "This one brilliant idea has caused us too much grief already. I prefer kissing to fighting."

"In that case," Bruce said, "you've come to the right partner in the Fowler and Patman love firm."

Lila giggled and fell back into Bruce's arms for a long, delicious kiss.

"Hi, Jess. It's me. Can you put Mom on?" Elizabeth asked, twisting her slender finger nervously around the cord of the outdoor pay phone. She pulled back her long blond ponytail, which was blowing across her face. The sea breeze was strong on the narrow pier off the Santa Carmine boardwalk, and the air was pungent with the scent of fish. Elizabeth's gaily flowered skirt fluttered around her legs.

All along the boardwalk groups of people milled around in their beachwear—shorts and T-shirts and bathing suits—browsing through the souvenir shops and playing the slot machines in the penny arcades. Barkers stood in front of their carnival games, delivering loud, colorful invitations meant to entice boyfriends to play for teddy bears and goldfish for their girlfriends. Rides were spinning and whirling to loud carnival music. But even from here Elizabeth could make out the distinctive, terrified screams of kids and adults alike as Santa Carmine's famous old wooden roller coaster swooped down its steep, rickety tracks.

As Elizabeth waited for her mother to come to the phone, she gazed over at Tom. He was sitting dejectedly on an old splintered bench, sandwiched in by two senior citizens in colorful Hawaiian shirts. She could tell how upset he was by his downcast eyes and furrowed brow. The traffic had been terrible, and when they'd finally arrived at the car-rental agency, the mysterious Carl Lister was long gone.

"No," the man behind the counter had said. He hadn't noticed a woman with Mr. Lister. With all the customers they'd had that morning, he'd told Elizabeth, he hadn't noticed much of anything. *Could Carl Lister have dropped poor Aunt Sylvia off somewhere between Sweet Valley and here?* Elizabeth wondered. She shuddered at the prospect. That would mean over a hundred miles that she and Tom would have to search.

"Let's face it, Liz," she whispered to herself, "this cover-up is history. You're going to have to tell Mom what's going on now."

Mrs. Wakefield's angry voice came on the line. "Where are you, young lady?" she cried. The wire was practically crackling from the tension in her mother's voice. "I've looked everywhere for you. I finally had to call over at the Egberts'. Winston told me you picked Tom up first thing this morning and headed off. That's the kind of selfish and irresponsible behavior I'd expect from your sister. Not from you."

"Mom," Elizabeth said, trying to head off the tirade. She had to come clean about Aunt Sylvia. But her mother wouldn't let her get a word in edgewise.

"And while you're off having fun, who do you think is supposed to be entertaining Aunt Sylvia? I called that hotel ten times this morning and I can't make heads or tails of what they're trying to tell me."

Elizabeth winced. Had her mother already found out that Aunt Sylvia was missing?

"I don't want Aunt Sylvia wandering around

that hotel all by herself," her mother went on. "Especially since they can't even keep track of their guests."

Whew! Apparently her mother assumed the hotel had goofed somehow. *Little did she know.*

Elizabeth gripped the phone tightly. "Mom, Mom, calm down. Everything's fine." She bit her lip. Her mother was already going ballistic. Telling her the truth about Aunt Sylvia now would be like putting nitroglycerin in a blender. *I can't do it,* Elizabeth thought. She motioned for Tom to come over.

"We're with Aunt Sylvia now," she told her mother cheerfully. "She wanted to spend the day at the beach. Here, I'll let you talk to her." Elizabeth shoved the phone at Tom.

"Hello there, dear," Tom said in his silly old-lady voice. "It's lovely to be back on the California coast. These two young whippersnappers have been so nice to show me around."

Elizabeth stifled a pained laugh and stared off down the pier toward the boardwalk. An elderly man was just turning the corner, heading away from them. Why did he seem so familiar looking? She pulled the picture of Aunt Sylvia and Uncle Howard out of her pocket. *Weird,* she thought. *He looks a little like Uncle Howard.* She stared after the man, but his face was obscured by his gray cap. *Gray cap?*

"Wait a minute," Elizabeth said to herself. "That's the same gray cap I saw on the man at the airport. Tom," she whispered furiously, "get off the phone."

"Got to go," Tom croaked, and hung up.

"What is it?" he asked, turning to face Elizabeth.

"Look," Elizabeth said, pointing at the old man. "I'm almost positive that's the same cap the man who grabbed Aunt Sylvia was wearing. And look at his face. He looks like Uncle Howard from the photo."

"Where?" Tom asked, looking around. "Isn't Uncle Howard dead?"

"There, there," she said, running toward the boardwalk, her heart pounding. She could hear Tom's footsteps trailing behind her.

But the closer they got, the more congested the busy boardwalk became. Daredevil teens cut them off, streaking past on Rollerblades; little kids stopped abruptly to take licks of their ice creams; and large groups of tourists lumbered by, walking side by side, blocking everybody's progress. And suddenly every old man seemed to be wearing a cap. Elizabeth twirled around in frustration. Where had he gone? How could he keep disappearing into thin air like that?

Tom came around her other side and shook his head. "No luck," he said. "I followed one gray cap through the crowd, but it turned out to be a woman. I'm sorry, Liz."

Elizabeth closed her eyes. "What are we going to do?" she moaned.

"Maybe we'd better get back."

"No," Elizabeth said emphatically. The man who had abducted Aunt Sylvia was here. She could feel it. And someone who looked an awful lot like her late uncle Howard was strolling the boardwalk, wearing the abductor's cap. She wasn't going anywhere until they'd solved this mystery.

Chapter Eight

"I haven't had this much fun since high school," Jessica gushed. She leaned forward in the cushioned red vinyl seat of a booth at the Dairi Burger soda shop in Sweet Valley. Deciding to play hooky with Mike from all that wedding work had been a stroke of genius. She smiled at him across the Formica-topped table and took a large sip from the thick, triple-chocolate shake they were sharing.

"I used to come to this soda shop every day after class with Lila and the gang from Sweet Valley High. Dairi Burger always had the best shakes."

Mike chuckled. "It takes me back a few years too. Only I was always outside leaning against a car."

Jessica played with the end of her straw. "I hope sitting inside isn't too tame for you," she teased.

She saw something flicker across Mike's amber eyes. Was it reluctance? He was out of his element, that was for sure.

"Not at all." Mike grinned at her. "Sharing a

shake with my favorite girl is just fine with me. Should we order some food?"

"Sure," Jessica said. She motioned for a waitress in a candy-cane-striped uniform. "Two Dairi Burger specials, please."

"What's that?" Mike asked.

Jessica winked. "You'll see."

"I can't wait," Mike said. "Since you picked it out, I'm sure I'll love it."

Jessica smiled. The whole day had been like that. Full of romantic high-school-type things. Everything Jessica wanted to do, they did. Everywhere she wanted to go, they went. They'd flown a kite in the park and then walked hand in hand to the pond and fed the ducks. They'd even gone on a ride on the old merry-go-round.

The waitress came by and put down two heaping platters of burgers with fries and onion rings.

Mike blinked his bright golden eyes in surprise. "You ate like this every day back in high school? How did you stay so thin?"

"It's my hot blood," Jessica teased in a sultry voice. "I burn calories faster than other women."

Mike nodded and bit into his hamburger, completely failing to raise so much as an eyebrow at her sexy innuendo.

Jessica felt vaguely disappointed. Once upon a time, Mike had responded to her flirting. *But come to think of it,* she thought, *he hasn't responded to anything I've done today.*

She had worn a short black miniskirt, and his eyes hadn't once gone below her waist. *Or above,* she thought, leaning over slightly in her low-cut scoop

148

neck to test the theory. Nope, he didn't blink an eye.

"Pass the ketchup, please?" Jessica asked throatily. She fluttered her long eyelashes ever so slightly.

When Mike handed it to her, she brushed his hand with her soft fingertips and gave him a steamy gaze.

He didn't seem to notice. Had she lost her impact on him?

Mike popped an onion ring into his mouth. "I'm having a really great time. Next we should take a drive down by the beach."

Now we're getting somewhere, Jessica thought. *What could be more sensual and romantic than rolling on the sand together with the waves crashing around us as the sun sets?*

"There's a new roller rink that just opened down there. That might be a lot of fun," Mike continued.

Jessica groaned. "This is like being with my brother," she muttered. She grabbed a fry and nibbled at the end. What had gotten into Mike? He even looked different. She glanced over at the stiff button-down shirt he was wearing. *I didn't even know he owned a shirt like that,* she thought. She studied it a little closer. Thin blue stripes lay against a white background. It was exactly like the one their mother had given Steven last Christmas. It even had a tear in the same . . . *Wait a minute!* Mike was wearing Steven's shirt!

Jessica let out a long sigh. *That's it,* she thought. *Mike's trying to act like Steven.*

"Mike," she said, smiling, "you can cut the act."

"What?" he asked innocently. He put down his hamburger and wiped his mouth. "What do you mean?"

149

"I mean," Jessica explained, "I already have a brother. I don't need another one. I like you just the way you are."

Mike grinned. "Which way is that, Jess?" he asked, the old sexiness creeping back into his voice.

Jessica widened her aquamarine eyes and smiled. He'd have to figure that one out for himself. But if her wishes came true, he'd go back to kissing her passionately the way he used to.

"Have you seen Steven?" Billie asked, stopping Isabella and Denise at the top of the Wakefields' thickly carpeted staircase. She pushed back a strand of her silky brown hair. "It's almost ten P.M. I've looked everywhere for him."

She'd gone through every single room in the sprawling Wakefield house, including the dank basement and the hot, musty attic. His car was in the gravel driveway, but nobody seemed to know where he was.

Isabella shook her long dark head of hair. "Did you try the living room?"

"Twice." Billie sighed. She'd even looked under the pale peach couch and matching love seat.

"How about the kitchen?" Denise asked, her button nose crinkling.

"Three times," Billie said with a groan. The brightly lit kitchen was equipped with every modern convenience, and even at this late hour it was filled with a crowd of catering employees, but no Steven. She gripped the wooden banister and sat down squarely at the top of the stairs.

150

Isabella sighed, her gray eyes darting around. "And he's not in his room?"

Billie shook her head wearily.

Isabella patted her shoulder. "We're calling it a night. But if we see him on our way to Alex's, we'll be sure to tell him that you're looking for him."

"Thanks," Billie murmured, shifting on the step to let the girls pass. She drew up her tanned legs, tucking her short olive green skirt around her, and rested her chin on her slim knees. *This is getting ridiculous,* she thought. *I have nowhere else to look.*

"Billie," Mrs. Wakefield called from the bottom of the stairs. "Have you decided on those songs yet?"

Billie winced. "Not yet," she called back. Yet another reason to find Steven.

"What about the flowers? Personally, I'd go with the pink-and-purple arrangement, but if you're still partial to white and yellow . . ."

Billie pulled herself up and walked down the steps toward Mrs. Wakefield. "I'm still waiting for Steven's input."

Mrs. Wakefield fingered her string of pearls. "If that's all"—she smiled—"I'm sure he'd agree with me. I'll just tell the florist we'd like the pink and purple."

I'm sure he'd agree with me, Billie thought with annoyance. She bit her lip. "I'd rather you didn't," she said, trying to keep the irritation out of her voice. "Steven should be along soon." She leaned against the banister.

"Okay, dear." Mrs. Wakefield shrugged, walking toward the kitchen. "But bear in mind we *are* running out of time."

Billie rolled her eyes. Didn't she know it. The

wedding was the day after tomorrow. "Steven!" she yelled for the umpteenth time. "Where are you?"

"Did you want me?" Steven asked sweetly, materializing as if out of thin air.

"Where have you been?" Billie blasted, whirling toward him. "I've looked everywhere for you. How could you run off and leave me like this? I'm tired and I want to go to bed. But there are a million things left to do and I can't do them all by myself. I can't believe how irresponsible and unavailable you're being."

"I understand your frustration," Steven intoned, his voice slow and measured. He smiled at her as if nothing in the world could ever bother him again. "I feel your pain. I'm glad you're able to share those feelings with me."

"What are you babbling about?" Billie fumed. A sheen of red rage began darkening her vision. "I'm really mad at you. You've made me crazy running around looking for you."

"No, Billie." Steven smiled. "No one makes anyone anything. You feel crazy. I, in turn, feel sad that you interpreted my actions in such a way that you chose to feel crazy."

Billie's mouth dropped. "Did you get hit on the head?" she asked. Maybe he had a concussion.

Steven chuckled happily. "Humor is a good way to defuse anger. That's very healthy. I see you're taking care of yourself."

Billie's eyes narrowed. She was going to take care of him in about two seconds with a right to the jaw. "We only have tomorrow left before the wedding." Her stomach tightened. "I need you to decide on some songs." She reached into her skirt pocket and with a shaking hand handed him the list of songs.

Steven took it and glanced down at the sheet of paper. "There are many choices here."

"Yes," Billie said between clenched teeth. "That's why we need to hurry up and make a decision."

Steven looked up and smiled at her. "I couldn't possibly," he stated simply. He handed her back the list. "Each song holds its own special meaning. If I pick one over another, that signals I feel one meaning has more importance. By tomorrow that may no longer be true for me."

The red in front of Billie's eyes was turning to a deep crimson. "Steven," she said, trying to mimic his own therapy speak. "I understand your reluctance."

"Thank you, Billie," Steven said, moving closer to her in the hallway.

"But," Billie went on, taking a step back from him. "It would mean a lot to me if you would help me narrow down the list."

Steven thought for a moment.

Probably listening for the alien's next instructions, she thought.

"Okay," Steven said, throwing his arm around her tensely hunched shoulders and giving her an affectionate squeeze. "I'll do my best. That's all any of us can ever truly do."

Billie nodded, gritting her teeth. "And the flowers," she ventured, "do you have any preference between the pink-and-purple or the white-and-yellow combination?" She knew she had to speak calmly. But on the other hand, time was running out. At any moment Steven might break into a Hare

153

Krishna chant, and then where would she be?

"No," Steven said finally, acting very pleased with himself. "I think in this case I can truly say I don't have a preference."

"Good," Billie said, shaking his arm off her. She'd tell Mrs. Wakefield they definitely preferred the white and yellow. "And your vows—how are you progressing?" She leaned against the hallway wall, her arms tightly crossed.

"My vows," Steven said slowly, enunciating each word. "Now that I've learned what relationships are all about, I feel I can begin to compose them."

Billie's eyes widened. "This is what you think relationships are about?" she gasped.

Steven nodded serenely and glided off toward Mr. Wakefield's den.

Billie shook her head. "I'm going to bed," she said with a groan. *But as soon as this wedding is over,* she promised herself, *I'm checking him into a loony bin.*

"Elizabeth, I'm about to collapse," Tom cried. Elizabeth turned. Tom had stopped in his tracks on the deserted Santa Carmine boardwalk and was resting his hands on his knees. The wooden slats at his feet were bathed in the placid red glow of the early morning sunrise. "Let's hold up a minute and think about what we're doing."

Tom looked up at her, and Elizabeth could see that his strong, handsome face was dulled by worry and exhaustion. He looked exactly like she felt.

They'd been on their feet almost the entire night, walking from one end of Santa Carmine to the other. They'd spent the wee hours between two and five

154

A.M. in the bright fluorescent light of a dingy all-night diner, hoping against hope that the old man with the gray cap would come in. But now the sun peeking out over the horizon seemed to mock them. Not only had the mysterious man with the gray cap and Uncle Howard's likeness disappeared, it seemed the rest of the world had too. The music from the amusement rides was silent and the barkers had all gone home, their carnival games shuttered and locked. Elizabeth looked down the long boardwalk as a lone early-bird jogger trudged past.

"He's not here," Tom said with a finality that chilled her to the bone.

Elizabeth nodded, her eyes welling up. They'd done their best, but that old man with the gray cap had still managed to slip through their fingers. And with him, so had all traces of Aunt Sylvia.

"You're right," Elizabeth said, hanging her head. "I just keep thinking that while we're turning one corner, he's going around the other. Like we're missing him by inches."

"I know how you feel," Tom said. "But we've done everything we can. He's not going to be walking around now. Everything is closed."

"But it will all open up again soon," Elizabeth said. She winced. Even she could hear the raw desperation in her voice.

Tom shook his head. "Liz, let it go. We don't have the manpower for this kind of search."

"Then we'll go to the police, Tom." She hadn't wanted to involve the Sweet Valley police because then her mother would find out they'd lost Aunt Sylvia for sure. But that didn't mean the Santa

155

Carmine police couldn't be brought in. "The police can put out an all-points bulletin and canvas the area properly. Maybe do a house-to-house search," she said, brightening. She began walking in the direction of a police station she'd noticed during the long night.

The police station was at the far end of the Santa Carmine boardwalk in an old red brick building. Elizabeth pushed through the thick glass door and walked up to a large wooden structure shaped like a big box, its finish dull and scratched. Behind it, towering high above them, sat a giant policeman in a rumpled blue uniform, a mug of steaming coffee practically lost in his thick hand.

Elizabeth cleared her throat. "Excuse me."

The desk sergeant looked them up and down. "What's the problem?" he asked in a gruff voice.

Elizabeth took a step forward. "We need some help in finding a missing person. My aunt Sylvia."

"Okay," the desk sergeant said, taking out a pen and a report form. "How long has she been missing?"

"Since yesterday," Elizabeth said. "We went to pick her up at the airport and I saw her being driven away in a rental car by a man in a gray cap. I think she may have been abducted."

"Was she struggling?" the desk sergeant asked.

Elizabeth thought back. "No," she said. "But she's in her seventies. She might not struggle if she knew she could be overpowered."

"And this man, did he seem like the overpowering type?"

"No, not exactly," Elizabeth said. "He looked to be in his seventies too."

The desk sergeant cracked an unpleasant smile and leaned back in his chair, his burly arms locked behind his head. "Are you sure they weren't *together*?" He laughed.

"They certainly were together," Elizabeth snapped, feeling her face heat up. "That's the problem. I was supposed to pick Aunt Sylvia up from the airport. Some strange man beat me to it, and I haven't heard from her since." *Why is this loser treating this like a joke?* Elizabeth fumed. *Doesn't he see that Aunt Sylvia's life could be in danger?*

The desk sergeant moved his massive frame forward again, the smirk on his face gone, at least for the moment. "Do you have a description of your aunt?"

Tom handed him the picture.

"They'd be older now," Elizabeth said. "Add about forty years."

"They?" the desk sergeant asked.

Elizabeth felt a scarlet blush creeping across her face. "That woman is my aunt Sylvia. But we think the man she's with looks a little like my uncle Howard there."

"Wait a minute! This man is married to this woman?" The desk sergeant stabbed a meaty finger at the picture, moving from the image of Uncle Howard to that of Aunt Sylvia. "So you're saying your uncle has abducted your aunt?"

"No!" Elizabeth screamed. "Her abductor just looks like Uncle Howard, only older. Forty years older, give or take. Because this man"—she pointed to the picture—"my uncle Howard, is dead."

The desk sergeant barely concealed the grin that was returning to his face. "Is this some sort of joke?

Some kind of college prank? Filing a false police report is a serious matter, you know."

"It isn't a joke," Tom cut in angrily. "We're just trying to find her aunt."

The desk sergeant shrugged his immense shoulders. "I'm sorry, but under the circumstances there's nothing we can do. Your aunt is a grown woman. There's no law against her getting into a car with a grown man. And frankly, at their age, I wouldn't worry too much."

"Won't you at least send out flyers with their descriptions?" Elizabeth pleaded.

"What descriptions?" He snorted. "They look like this, only add forty years? Who would see the similarity?"

"I certainly did," Elizabeth said. "I picked Aunt Sylvia out right away."

"Uh-huh," the desk sergeant scoffed, "and your dead uncle, too."

Elizabeth's mouth dropped. She couldn't believe this! He wasn't taking them seriously at all. He was treating them like a couple of crazy kids. She *had* seen Aunt Sylvia. And Uncle Howard, too. *Oh no! Uncle Howard? Maybe I am going crazy*, she thought.

"Come on," Tom said, pulling her arm. "Let's get back to Sweet Valley. We're both exhausted and we have a long ride home."

Elizabeth sighed. Tom was right. They'd done as much as they could in this town. Wherever Aunt Sylvia was now, they weren't going to find her this way.

Chapter
Nine

Tom cruised at a steady fifty-five miles an hour down the sparsely populated highway toward Sweet Valley. The morning sun they'd seen rise over the Santa Carmine boardwalk at daybreak was higher in the sky now, but it still wasn't rush hour. He and Elizabeth seemed to be the only ones on the road besides a few long-haul truckers.

Tom glanced over at the bundle huddled against the passenger's side of the Jeep. "Are you asleep?" he whispered.

Elizabeth stirred. "No. I'm just cold." She pulled her long flowered skirt tighter around her legs.

Tom turned the heat up another notch.

"I can't stop seeing that old man's face in my mind." Elizabeth shuddered. "Those eyes, just like Uncle Howard's."

Tom shrugged. "He was an old man, Liz. He just looked like an aged version of the photo. Who knows what Uncle Howard would really look like now? Maybe nothing like the picture."

"No," Elizabeth insisted. "His face was so distinctive."

"Liz," Tom said, maneuvering the Jeep into the fast lane to pass a slow-moving milk truck. "You're tired."

Elizabeth's bottom lip trembled. "I know what I saw."

Tom sighed. *This is nuts,* he thought. All this sneaking around was turning Elizabeth into a wreck. Now she was thinking she'd seen her dead uncle Howard.

"Liz, are you saying you actually saw Uncle Howard? Because if you are, then you're saying he's back from the dead and has spirited away your aunt Sylvia. You're seriously weirding me out now."

Elizabeth sat up, her eyes brimming with tears. "Well, I'm sorry you feel that way." Her voice quavered. "But it upsets me too."

Tom gritted his teeth and checked his rearview mirror. There was a large diesel barreling down behind him. He signaled and crossed to the middle lane. "Don't you think it's possible that you're upset *because* you're seeing things?"

Elizabeth stayed silent.

"You couldn't have seen Uncle Howard," Tom went on. "It's impossible. Even in your family."

"What's that supposed to mean?" Elizabeth asked sharply, shifting in her seat.

Tom sighed. "Well . . . a lot of strange stuff seems to happen to the Wakefields that doesn't happen to anyone else I know."

"Are you saying it's because of my family?" Elizabeth asked. There was a chill to her tone.

"Not necessarily your family," Tom said. "Maybe any family." Not that anything like this had ever happened in his family.

Elizabeth crossed her arms and settled farther away from him in her seat. "So you're blaming families in general."

Maybe I am, Tom thought. "All I know is that being on my own, I don't have all these problems."

Elizabeth narrowed her eyes. "I see what you're getting at. You're saying that when you're alone, you don't have to worry about anyone else."

"Right," Tom said. Now she was seeing his point.

"Well, that's what families are about," Elizabeth snapped.

"Problems?" Tom asked.

Elizabeth threw up her hands. "No . . . yes . . . sometimes." She sighed deeply. "It's about sticking together when problems come up. It's about being there for each other."

Tom raised his eyebrows. "I don't know," he muttered. "Maybe family life isn't as wonderful as I thought."

"Let's do it," Bruce said, holding Lila's soft hand tightly as they walked down the long carpeted hallway of the law offices of Ballard, Smythe, Loeb & Hobbs for their early morning appointment. In a minute they would be meeting their lawyers in one of the darkly paneled conference rooms. *Then we'll be able to put this whole pre-engagement prenuptial agreement ordeal behind us,* Bruce thought.

"I'm a little nervous," Lila said, straightening the lapel on her tan linen jacket.

Bruce squeezed her hand. "No reason to be," he said. "They're professionals. This will go smoothly." The agreements were probably all drawn up. The lawyers would walk him and Lila through the documents and then they'd sign and be done with it.

"I'm just afraid they're going to think we're foolish for not having written our own agreement," Lila said. "It probably took them ten minutes."

Bruce shrugged. "They probably worked on it for at least a half an hour. They get paid by the quarter hour, you know."

"I guess they're not getting much from us, then." Lila laughed.

Bruce kissed her on the nose. "Whatever we're paying them is worth it. Because it means we don't have to fight."

Lila winked at him. "I like your generous attitude."

Bruce felt his stomach start to flutter. "Lila, please. I'm helpless around a woman who winks."

Lila grinned. "I'll remember that for future negotiations."

Bruce opened the conference-room door wide to usher Lila in.

"Oh no," Bruce heard Lila scream.

Bruce walked in behind her. *What's going on in here? It's like World War III!*

"Duck, Lila," Bruce shouted as a heavy law book went flying over their heads.

Mr. Loeb grabbed another one and lobbed it

across the conference table at Ms. Taylor-Hobbs. "I'll drum you out of the profession before I make one more concession!"

Ms. Taylor-Hobbs in turn grabbed a handful of legal documents and threw them up in the air. "This is what I think of your proposals." Paper fluttered down around them.

Lila jumped back with a yelp and hid behind Bruce. "What are they doing?" she gasped.

"Negotiating, it seems," Bruce said, blocking a flying legal pad with his arm.

"We will not give you a penny more," Ms. Taylor-Hobbs screamed. "I don't care what you say."

"Well, you can forget the car and the beach house in Malibu!" Mr. Loeb shouted.

"Malibu?" Lila asked, cowering behind Bruce.

Bruce shrugged. "I guess it's hypothetical."

"In that case," Ms. Taylor-Hobbs shrieked, "we want the jewelry, the main house, and double the alimony."

"Well," Mr. Loeb shouted back, "we want triple all your savings!"

"That's impossible," Ms. Taylor-Hobbs screeched, hurling her briefcase at him. "We want two-thirds of everything you make."

Mr. Loeb grabbed a dark green jacket off the back of one of the conference chairs that ringed the table. He threw it down on the floor and stomped on it. "That's what we think about your two-thirds!"

"That's my jacket!" Ms. Taylor-Hobbs lunged for him, grabbed the front of his starched white shirt, and wrestled him to the ground.

Bruce pulled Lila to safety and slammed the

conference door behind them. *Not that they would have heard us,* he thought. "So much for coming to an easy agreement," he said with a smirk. "They're fighting over money that's not even theirs!"

Lila grabbed his arm. "Let's get out of here. I've had enough of pre-engagement prenuptial battles."

"I'm with you, Lila." Bruce steered her past the rows of secretaries whose desks lined the way to the front door of the law offices.

A young receptionist with teased auburn hair jumped up and held open the door. "All through?" she asked.

"You can say that again!" Bruce shouted as they barreled through the entrance and made for the elevators. "But you'd better call an ambulance for conference room C. Somebody's gonna get hurt in there."

Elizabeth stepped out of the passenger side of the Jeep onto the gravel driveway of 72 Calico Drive. Her legs wobbled beneath her like two bowls of Jell-O, and for a minute she wondered how she would ever make it to the front door. The Wakefields' white colonial-style house, always so welcoming, loomed ahead of her imposingly. Its green shuttered windows squinting accusingly at her through the late morning sun. *Day three and your aunt Sylvia is still missing!* the house seemed to say.

Elizabeth groaned. "What am I going to tell my mother, Tom?"

Tom came around from the other side of the Jeep, pushing his dark brown hair from the worried lines of his forehead. "I don't know. But you can't tell her that Uncle Howard abducted Aunt Sylvia."

Elizabeth sighed. Her body was screaming for sleep, her mind was exhausted. "I don't know what else to tell her."

"That guy just looks like Uncle Howard," Tom pointed out. "It can't actually be him. There's no such thing as ghosts."

Elizabeth slumped against the side of the Jeep. The warm metal felt wonderful against her back. She longed for sleep. "Maybe Uncle Howard has a twin brother," she suggested.

Tom shook his head and leaned against the Jeep beside her. "You'd know that. Uncle Howard is . . . er, *was* a member of your family."

Elizabeth shuddered, her whole body shaking. "I don't know what to do," she cried. "This is so crazy. I can't make any sense of it."

Tom wrapped her in his arms. "It's okay, it's okay," he whispered, rocking her back and forth. "We'll get to the bottom of it."

Elizabeth buried her head in Tom's chest. His body felt warm and comforting. She could smell the sea air in his polo shirt. "Here I thought we were such supersleuths," she mumbled.

Tom gently stroked her hair that had fallen out of her ponytail. "Don't give up hope, Liz. We have one more day."

Elizabeth looked up at him, her bottom lip trembling. "That's what I'm worried about. What if we don't find her? I thought this would be simple." She squeezed back her tears. "It's got me completely stumped. We're no match for

165

an uncle who's returned from the dead."

Tom began to twitch. "We've got to stop thinking that way," he said, his voice agitated. "It only upsets us. I'm sure there's a logical explanation."

Elizabeth wrapped her arms around him. "You're right." Now it was her turn to calm Tom down. "We're tired. Our nerves are shot."

"Sleep," Tom said. "That's what we both need. We'll feel better after a few hours of sleep."

Elizabeth leaned against him for the last few steps to her front door.

"Do you want me to come in?" he asked.

Elizabeth looked up into his tired dark eyes. Some of the things he'd said in the beginning of the drive about family life and how it wasn't worth the bother had really upset her. *But he's still Tom,* she reminded herself. And whether he realized it or not, he was there for her and he always had been. Which was exactly what families were all about. *I have to remember to tell him that,* she thought. *And I will, when things get sorted out.*

"Sure," Elizabeth said. "I'll make you a nice quiet breakfast."

She pushed open the front door, and they stepped inside to find the house in a state of total chaos.

"I don't know, Frankie," Winston heard the tent man say. He was holding up a pole in the Wakefields' backyard. "It doesn't look right to me."

"What do you mean?" his helper said.

"I mean, you'd have to be the size of a mouse to get in here."

166

"What's going on?" Winston asked.

"Nothing," the tent man said. "We're just having a little technical difficulty."

Winston grabbed the plans from the man's hand and looked at them. *Great,* he thought as he turned them right-side up. Mr. Wakefield had personally put him in charge of the tent men.

"This is all wrong," he said, studying the plan. "These marks mean yards, not feet. And these mean inches, not yards." At this rate half the tent was going to end up in the neighbor's yard while the guests would practically have to do the limbo to get into the rest of it.

"Let me see that," the tent man said. "Hey, Frankie, I think he's right."

"You guys better rip everything down and start over again," Winston said. "I only hope we get it done on time."

Jessica stepped out onto the back porch in her hottest new bikini. She had time for a dip in the pool before her lunch date with Mike. She felt a twinge of guilt about skipping out on yet another afternoon of wedding preparations, but everything here was under control, wasn't it? Except for those men throwing around the tent poles. . . .

"Oh, well," she murmured to herself, "it isn't my concern." She just wanted to relax and enjoy a quick swim.

She stepped up to the pool. *Wait a minute,* she thought, looking over the edge. *What's wrong with this picture?* The water was pink! And it was turning pinker by the second.

167

"Hey," Jessica called out. "This water's been contaminated."

"No, no, young lady," the pool consultant said, strolling across the yard. "We use only the finest chlorine supplements to get a sparkling blue color."

"What do you call that?" Jessica demanded, pointing at the water.

The pool consultant looked down and screamed in shock. "It's red!"

"Fuchsia is more like it, actually," Jessica said, crossing her arms. "And you'd better do something about it. Quick."

"Did you see what they did to the pool?" Jessica asked, stepping into the back hallway.

"No," Billie said, ducking through the doorway to the dining room. And she didn't want to see, either. She *wanted* to find some quiet place away from the chaos for a few minutes. "That's all I need," Billie said to herself. "Please let me find a little peace."

She opened door after door only to find people involved in frantic activity. Finally she switched on the lights of the Wakefields' TV room. Empty. *Thank goodness.* She sat down and began to massage her temples. But immediately the door was flung open. She scrunched down. *Maybe they won't see me,* she thought. *Maybe they'll go away.* No such luck.

Alexandra and Noah stomped into the room, their voices rising angrily.

"I never said I didn't like your dress, Alex."

Alexandra turned her slender back to him, her

fists clenched at her sides. "You implied it."

Noah grabbed her arm and twirled her around to face him. "You're a mind reader now?"

Alexandra shook herself free and stepped back, her dark green eyes flashing. "I don't have to be," she threatened. "It was written all over your face."

Noah scowled and crossed his athletic arms. "Sure you're not exaggerating again?"

Alexandra's pretty face flushed. "With the smirk you gave me?" she shouted.

Billie jumped up from her hiding place. "I can't take it anymore!" she screamed. She ran from the room, leaving the shocked faces of Noah and Alexandra behind her.

"Billie," Elizabeth cried as Billie ran past, practically knocking Tom over on their way toward the kitchen. "Are you all right?"

"I'll be fine," Billie shouted back. "If I can find a moment of peace." Elizabeth watched as Billie sprang up the staircase, taking the steps two at a time.

"It looks like we're not the only crazed ones," Elizabeth said.

Tom nodded. "I hope it's safe to go in the kitchen."

"Better be." Elizabeth smiled. "I promised you breakfast."

They stepped into the room to see Denise's slender frame covered in flour, frantically throwing food around. Her pale, flawless skin was smudged with mustard and her dark glossy hair was matted with blueberry jam. She was pouring melted cheese on strawberries and squeezing whipped cream onto crackers.

"What are you doing?" Elizabeth gasped.

"The caterer's last clients came down with food poisoning," Denise cried. "The caterer has skipped town. I'm in charge of hors d'oeuvres."

Elizabeth's mouth dropped. "Were those his recipes? No wonder they got sick."

"No," Denise wailed. "But this is all I know how to make. I'm helpless around the kitchen."

Elizabeth took the bowl of orange liquid from her hands. "Why don't you go help Isabella and Danny," she suggested firmly, ushering Denise out. "I think they're in the living room tidying up."

"Let me do it," Isabella ordered with a toss of her head. She grabbed the vacuum cleaner from Danny. "Even in heels I can do this faster than you."

"Be my guest," Danny said, stepping back. "But it's harder than it looks. You have to watch out for the—"

In a blink of an eye the vacuum cleaner sucked up the corner of Mrs. Wakefield's expensive oriental rug.

"Danny, pull," Isabella shrieked, "or we'll lose the whole thing."

Danny dived to his knees and wrestled with the living-room rug with all his might. "Turn it off, turn it off!" he screamed.

Isabella gripped the switch, yanking it toward her, but it broke off in her hand. "I can't," she cried. "It's out of control."

The vacuum cleaner made a loud gurgle as it swallowed the rest of the rug. An ominous sound began to emanate from the motor.

"It's going to blow," Danny shouted as he fell to the floor. "Hit the deck!"

Isabella dived behind the pale peach couch just as the vacuum cleaner reached the meltdown point. The top blew open, blasting clouds of dirt and dust all over the living room. It covered the couch, the love seat, and especially them. "What are we going to tell Mrs. Wakefield?" she screamed.

Lila reached the front door of the Wakefields' house at the same time as the delivery boy from the dry cleaner. *Boom!* A huge explosion had sounded from inside the house.

"What was that?" Lila asked.

"Sounded like a firecracker," the boy said.

More like a bomb, Lila thought. "Who ever heard of firecrackers at a wedding?"

The boy shrugged. "Do you want to take this?" he asked. He held out a long white dress wrapped in cellophane. Billie's wedding dress.

"Sure," Lila said. "Do they owe you anything for the cleaning?"

"Nah, it's on the house," the boy said nervously. "It was just a quick press. We didn't touch it. I swear."

Lila lifted the plastic bag from around the dress. "I'll just have a look." There was something about the sound of the delivery boy's voice she didn't like.

"Got to go," the boy yelped, jumping off the stoop and running toward his bicycle.

"Oh no!" Lila screamed, staring down at the dress. "There's a big stain on the back. Hey, you, get back here."

But the boy was long gone, pedaling furiously down the street.

"What a disaster," Lila said, walking into the house. "How am I going to tell Billie?"

Steven held up his hand as Lila walked up to him in his father's den. "I'm on the phone," he mouthed. Lila looked as upset as Mrs. Winkler sounded on the other end of the phone. But he was getting used to that. He channeled his concentration back to the phone.

"Steven, are you there?" Mrs. Winkler asked.

"Yes," Steven said. "I'm here."

"Do you understand what I'm saying?" Mrs. Winkler asked. "Because it doesn't seem to be sinking in."

"Yes, yes," Steven said over the phone. "I understand. You and your husband can't get a flight out of Mexico to make the wedding."

"Because of the hurricane damage, the first flight isn't until next week," Mrs. Winkler said.

"Yes, Mrs. Winkler," Steven said. "It is very sad. You could even call it tragic."

"Are you all right?" Mrs. Winkler asked. "Because you're acting very strange. I thought you'd be upset."

"No, not anymore," Steven said. "Those sorts of negative emotions are all behind me now."

"I'm going to get off, Steven," Mrs. Winkler said. "I think this is a bad connection. I'll call Billie later."

Steven hung up and glided toward the hall. It was fate, after all. Billie's parents weren't meant to be at their wedding. Otherwise there wouldn't have been a hurricane in Mexico and their flight wouldn't have been canceled. *Therefore,* he thought, *there's nothing to be upset about.*

He smiled. Since he'd learned to understand his emotions from those self-help books, things like this didn't bother him. He had evolved to a higher plane.

Mike pulled up on his motorcycle. "Hey, what are you doing?" he yelled. Some joker in a beat-up VW bug was grinding his gears outside the Wakefields' house. The car stalled in the driveway.

The guy poked out his head. "I can't keep it going."

Mike recognized him. He was one of Jessica's friends. "It's Winston, isn't it?"

"Yeah," Winston said. "I think it's the clutch."

Mike stood over the VW's engine compartment and sniffed. "That's not the problem," he said. "You flooded the engine."

Winston gave him a sheepish grin. "I'm always doing that."

"Well, give it a rest," Mike said. "Then back up slowly."

Winston jammed his foot on the gas and popped the clutch. The car lurched forward onto the yard, shuddered, and died.

Mike walked over, shaking his head. "I said slowly and backward." He bent under the VW to see the damage. The car looked fine, but it had run over a long power line. "What's this?" he asked, holding up the snapped cable.

Winston grimaced. "It's supposed to be connected to that thing," he said, pointing to the nearby generator. "That's where the electricity for the backyard comes from."

Would have come from. Mike groaned inwardly. "Put the car in neutral," he grumbled. "And then get back here and help me push."

"There you are," Elizabeth said. "I've been looking all over for you."

Jessica turned to see Elizabeth running down the hall toward her.

"What is it, Liz?" she asked, stepping into her bedroom. "I've got to get dressed. Mike should be here any minute."

"The milliner is downstairs," Elizabeth said. "She needs to see our bridesmaid dresses to match the ribbon for our hats with the buttons on the dresses."

"You mean they're not here?" Jessica asked. "Val should have brought them hours ago."

Elizabeth dropped down onto Jessica's bright apple green bedspread. "Well, she hasn't. But that's okay. Just tell me what color they are."

"I don't know." Jessica groaned. "I left it up to Val to decide what buttons to use."

Elizabeth made a face. "Then you'd better get on the phone with her."

Jessica grabbed her princess phone and punched out the studio's number. "There's no answer."

"Keep trying," Elizabeth said, hoisting herself

up and starting for the door. "Or we're going to look pretty ridiculous. We'll end up with pink hats when we should have blue ones."

Well, at least we'll match the pool, Jessica thought.

Mike knocked on the Wakefields' front door. No answer. He knocked again. Still no answer. Finally he just opened it up. "Man," he said to himself, jumping out of the way as people ran past him screaming. "What is this, the running of the bulls? Hey, Jess!" he called out, hoping she'd appear soon. He didn't want to go wandering around looking for her in this madhouse.

I'll take a seat in the living room, he thought. *That's where dates usually wait.* "Whoa," he said to himself, surveying the mess. There was dirt and dust all over the place. "Mrs. Wakefield isn't much of a homemaker. Maybe they should think about hiring a maid." He stepped back into the foyer.

"Michael," Mr. Wakefield said, coming up behind him.

Mike spun around. "Mr. Wakefield, nice to see you again."

"Here to see Jessica?" Mr. Wakefield asked.

"That's right, sir," Mike said. A few "sirs" never hurt anyone, he'd always thought. Especially when you were trying to make a good impression on someone's parents.

"Seeing that you're the best man, I think you should hold on to these rings," Mr. Wakefield said, reaching into his pocket. "They were my

175

grandparents'. I think they'll make lovely wedding rings for Steven and Billie."

"I'd be honored, sir."

"Hmm," Mr. Wakefield said, "they must be in the other pocket." He started patting himself down and turning out each pocket.

"Maybe they're in another pair of pants," Mike said, trying to be helpful.

Mr. Wakefield scratched his head. "I just had them." He looked around the room. "Oh, I know, I put them in my cardigan. Take a seat in the living room. I'll go get it."

That's okay, Mike thought. "You go ahead. I'll be here."

Mr. Wakefield returned in a few moments. In his hand was his gray cardigan, his finger poking out of a big hole in its pocket. "I'm afraid I'm in trouble."

That's for sure, Mike thought. *With the mess I've seen so far, you'll be lucky if you can find the floor.*

"Liz," Mrs. Wakefield called, catching up with Elizabeth on the back porch.

Elizabeth winced. She'd been trying to avoid her mother all day. It was bad enough she'd lost Aunt Sylvia without her mother fawning over her. It made her feel even more guilty.

"Let me take a look at you," Mrs. Wakefield said, grabbing Elizabeth by both her hands. "I can't tell you how much easier it is for me seeing your helpful face."

If Elizabeth could have sunk into the ground at that moment, she gladly would have.

"Without you, I would never have the strength

176

to continue with this," Mrs. Wakefield said. She pulled Elizabeth toward her and gave her a big hug.

Elizabeth tried to wriggle free. "You're doing fine, Mom. You don't need me or anyone else."

Mrs. Wakefield tightened her clasp. "No, that's why I have to keep telling you over and over again how much I depend on you."

"Mom, please," Elizabeth said, struggling harder. "Everyone is helping." *How can I get her to stop?* she thought. *She's making me crazy.*

Mrs. Wakefield squeezed her once more and then let go. "Oh, Elizabeth, you're so modest."

No, I'm not, Elizabeth thought through clenched teeth. *And when you find out what's happened to Aunt Sylvia, I won't be surprised if you disown me!*

"Oh, Billie," Mrs. Wakefield said, walking into the den a few minutes later.

Billie opened her eyes. She was curled up in a cushy floral-patterned armchair, futilely massaging her temples against a headache that would probably never go away.

"I spoke to the florist. I ordered the pink-and-purple flowers. So we can cross that off the list."

Billie grimaced, the pain in her head suddenly increasing. *Why is this happening to me?* she thought. "I wanted the white-and-yellow flowers."

"No," Mrs. Wakefield said with a pleasant smile. "We discussed this last night. Don't you remember? Whatever Steven wanted, we were going to get."

"Steven," Billie said between gritted teeth, "was fine with the white-and-yellow."

"I spoke to him, dear," Mrs. Wakefield said, an edge creeping into her voice. "He said the pink-and-purple were fine."

Billie jumped to her feet. "Steven!" she yelled. She turned to Mrs. Wakefield. "As soon as he gets here, I'm sure we'll get this straightened out."

Steven glided into the room, smiling benignly.

"Darling," Mrs. Wakefield said, "didn't you just tell me that pink-and-purple flowers would be fine with you?"

"Yes," Steven said.

"Steven," Billie said, placing her hands on her hips. "Didn't you tell me last night white-and-yellow were fine?"

"Yes," he said.

"Well, which is it?" Billie's head started throbbing in double time. "You have to pick one or the other."

"They're both fine," Steven said.

Billie rolled her eyes. They weren't going to get anywhere with him. This was maddening. She was going to end up with a flower scheme she detested because Steven refused to get involved.

"Steven," Billie said, "you have to take a stand."

Steven shrugged. "I'm sorry, Billie, but I no longer adhere to conflict."

Billie could feel her face heating up. She stretched her long fingers to keep them from clenching into fists. "What is that supposed to mean? We're trying to decide on the color scheme of our wedding."

"It's okay, Billie," Mrs. Wakefield said. "I'll call the florist back. After all, it is your wedding."

"Thank you," Billie said as Mrs. Wakefield left the den. She collapsed back into the chair, glaring at Steven. *It is my wedding,* she thought. *But it's supposed to be Steven's, too.* She turned to him. "What's gotten into you?" she demanded. "You knew I wanted the white-and-yellow flowers and your mother wanted the pink-and-purple ones. Why didn't you back me up? You're acting like you don't care about our wedding."

"Conflict is a toxic state," Steven stated calmly. "I refuse to be drawn into it."

Billie's dark blue eyes blazed at him. "Instead you left *us* to fight it out."

Steven shifted his feet. "You both chose to assign importance to something I chose not to."

"Stop it, Steven!" Billie insisted. "You're driving me crazy with that talk. These are decisions someone has to make. And if you helped, it would make it a lot less stressful."

"Stress is another toxic state I refuse to be drawn into."

Billie grabbed a plump downy pillow from the chair next to hers and used it to muffle a long, savage scream. Then she set the pillow neatly aside. "Okay, I'm calm now," she said, concentrating on her breathing. "Have you written your vows?"

Steven smiled happily and produced a long yellow legal pad.

Billie took it from him and leaned back against her chair. She started turning page after page. Each one was filled with Steven's tight, spidery handwriting.

179

There were also scattered diagrams, charts, and even a few statistical equations.

"What's this?" she gasped.

"My notes," Steven said, looking very pleased with himself. "I've made a careful study—"

"We need vows, Steven," Billie interrupted. "Words that we're going to say to each other tomorrow. Promises we're going to make in front of a yard full of people. These"—she threw the notebook at his head—"are not vows." She gripped the cushioned armrests of the chair.

"Before the end of the day," she continued, her voice calm and measured despite the roaring in her brain, "I want you to write one page. That's 250 words or fewer that can be read at the ceremony. Do you understand?"

Steven nodded and picked up his legal pad.

"Please do it now," she said sternly.

He turned and walked out of the room.

When he was gone, Billie again reached for the pillow beside her. Another nice long scream might do her good.

Chapter
Ten

"That's just what I needed," Elizabeth said to herself, stepping out of the steaming bathroom in her white terry-cloth robe. "A nice hot shower." She adjusted the yellow towel wrapped around her head and started down the hallway.

Earlier in the afternoon she'd taken a quick catnap. Now, as she returned to her bedroom, things felt almost back to normal. *But not quite,* she grimly reminded herself. Aunt Sylvia was still missing. And, she thought, shuddering, the mysterious Uncle Howard look-alike was still lurking around. But even that didn't seem so bad now that she was refreshed. She sat on her bed and began to towel dry her long blond hair.

There was a rap at the door. Jessica stuck in her head. "Are you busy?" she asked.

"No," Elizabeth said. "I just had a long, luxurious shower."

"I was wondering where all the fog came from," Jessica joked. "I thought it might be a low cloud formation." She flopped down on Elizabeth's lavender bedspread.

"What's up?" Elizabeth asked. "How was your lunch with Mike?" She worked her tortoiseshell comb through a tough tangle in her hair.

"Fine," Jessica said dreamily. She rolled over and looked at Elizabeth. "You should use a conditioner."

Elizabeth tugged at a knot. "I did."

"Here, let me do it." Jessica took the comb and knelt above her sister, skillfully moving the comb through her tangles.

Elizabeth laughed. Her twin always had been more expert at beauty matters.

"Do you know what we're doing about the rehearsal dinner?" Jessica asked.

"No." Elizabeth groaned. "I forgot all about that. I guess since we're the groom's family, we're supposed to arrange it."

"It's too much," Jessica said. She turned Elizabeth's head to work on the other side. "Do you think we should wear French twists?" She piled Elizabeth's hair on top of her head.

"Jessica," Elizabeth said, smiling and shaking her hair free. "What should we do about the rehearsal dinner?"

Her sister stood up and walked over to the mirror. She twisted her golden hair and studied her profile. "I don't think even Mom could plan another thing."

"You're right," Elizabeth said, getting up. As it was, their mother was on overload. "I'm going to ask Dad what he thinks."

Jessica shrugged and let her hair drop. "I guess a French twist won't work with those hats."

Elizabeth walked down the hall to her parents' bedroom. Her father was pulling out the drawers of his tall mahogany chest and emptying them onto the carpeted floor.

"Dad?" Elizabeth asked. "What are you doing?"

"Hmm?" He looked up distractedly.

Elizabeth pointed to the pile of clothing.

"Oh," her father said. "I seem to have misplaced Steven's and Billie's wedding rings."

"Do you need help?" Elizabeth asked, looking at the mess.

"No, no," he said, sifting through the clothes. "I'm just retracing all the day's movements."

Elizabeth stifled a laugh. "I didn't know you were in the habit of dumping out your drawers on a regular basis."

He looked at her, perplexed, and then laughed. "This is how I found them in the first place, silly," he said. "They were your great-grandparents'."

"Oh." Elizabeth nodded sagely. As if that explained anything.

Mr. Wakefield made a face at her. "I stored them in one of these drawers. I just can't remember which one."

Elizabeth smirked. "Oh, good thinking, Dad."

"Stop teasing." He grinned. "Before I put you to work."

Elizabeth giggled and leaned against the doorframe. "Are we having a rehearsal dinner?"

"Oh, right," Mr. Wakefield said, putting his hand to his head. "That's our responsibility, isn't it?"

183

"I guess so." Elizabeth crossed her arms over her terry-cloth robe. "But under the circumstances . . ."

"You're right," Mr. Wakefield said, shaking his head. "It's too much. I don't want your mother getting involved in anything else."

"That's what I thought," Elizabeth said. "Maybe we should forget about it. I don't think anyone will even notice."

"No," Mr. Wakefield said. "We'll do something." He reached into his back pocket and took out his wallet. "Here's a credit card," he said, handing her one. "Take Steven and Billie, your sister, Michael, and Tom out to dinner. Alfredo's is a good restaurant. It's right in the hotel where Aunt Sylvia is staying."

Not Aunt Sylvia, Elizabeth thought.

"I know you've been seeing a lot of her," Mr. Wakefield continued. "But maybe you could drop in on her while you're there. Mother tells me she adores you and Tom."

"Sure, Dad," Elizabeth said, her good mood evaporating. *Who knows?* she thought. *Maybe I'll find Aunt Sylvia at the hotel and this will all turn out to have been a terrible mistake.* Well, she could always hope.

"Alfredo's is a great idea," Tom said, scanning the well-heeled patrons, all in fancy dresses or jackets and ties, as he and Elizabeth entered the elegant Italian restaurant. It seemed to Tom as if a lot of the hotel's guests were dining there, sitting comfortably in their plush red chairs at the linen-covered tables.

He was glad he'd had a chance to grab a few winks and freshen up after his and Elizabeth's all-nighter at Santa Carmine. His decision to exchange his khakis and polo shirt for a dark blue blazer, gray striped tie, and dress slacks had been the right move too. Alfredo's definitely had a dress code.

He reached over and squeezed Elizabeth's hand. She looked beautiful with her golden hair worn loose, sweeping across her bare shoulders that rose gracefully from her midnight blue stretch-satin dress. "Maybe Aunt Sylvia is eating here right now," he offered hopefully.

Elizabeth shook her head, her blond hair shimmering in the restaurant's candlelight. "I called the concierge just before we left my parents' house. Still no word from her."

"Can I help you?" the maître d' asked, gliding up to them in an immaculate black tux with a purple bow tie.

"We have a reservation," Tom said. "The name is Wakefield. Table for six."

"I believe the rest of your party is here," the maître d' said. "One moment, please."

Elizabeth turned to Tom as the maître d' scanned his list. "What if Jess or Steven wants to see Aunt Sylvia?" she asked.

"There we are," the maître d' said. "Table ten. This way, please."

Tom followed Elizabeth and the maître d' toward a long rectangular table by the large front window. He could see Jessica, wearing a black halter dress and pearl drop earrings, in deep conversation with Mike, her bare arm entwined in his. Steven was leaning back in his chair, eyes slightly glazed. Both Mike and Steven were wearing navy blue sport jackets and colorful ties. Billie had pulled back her dark brown hair with a blue velvet ribbon and was studying the menu.

"I don't think we have to worry about that," Tom whispered to Elizabeth. "Aunt Sylvia is probably the last person on their minds right now."

Elizabeth sighed. "I'm sure you're right. I wish I could say the same thing."

"What's right?" Jessica asked, extracting her arm from Mike's.

"This setting," Elizabeth said breezily. "You all look so happy and relaxed."

Tom winked at her. Elizabeth was always the diplomat.

A carbon copy of the maître d', this one with a blue bow tie, came up to their table. He handed Tom and Elizabeth each a menu.

"The specials," he announced, "are brook trout almandine, lobster bisque, and filet mignon with a dash of sherry."

"That sounds great," Tom said. His mouth was already watering.

"Which one?" Elizabeth asked.

"All of them." Tom laughed. "I'm starving."

"Me too," Billie said. "I was so busy this afternoon, I forgot to eat." She closed her menu and turned to Steven. "What are you going to have?"

Tom looked over at Steven. He still had that glazed look in his eyes. Maybe he was starving too.

"Nothing," Steven said, closing his menu.

"There are no macrobiotic foods on the menu."

Tom gave a start. "Macrobiotic? Since when did you go macrobiotic?" He could remember quite clearly Steven devouring a ham-and-cheese sandwich at the surprise engagement party.

"Since five minutes ago," Billie said angrily. "Steven doesn't even know what macrobiotic eating is. He's just being difficult. Like he's been for the past few days."

Elizabeth leaned forward. "Billie, I'm sure Steven has a better reason than that."

"It's just nerves," Mike offered. "The guy is going through a hard time."

Billie glared.

"What's that supposed to mean?" Jessica asked.

Tom winced. *Better tread carefully, Mike,* he thought. If there was one thing he'd learned about the Wakefield twins, it was that they couldn't stand sexist comments.

"I mean," Mike said, slapping Steven on the back, "it's a big step. He's giving up his freedom. You know, taking on the old ball and chain. He's bound to feel a little nauseous."

Tom cringed, wishing he could hide under the table. He didn't want to witness Elizabeth and Jessica ripping Mike's head off.

"And what about Billie?" Jessica asked, her eyes flashing. "It's not a big step for her? She's also giving up her freedom."

Mike shrugged, looking over at Tom for support. Tom shook his head. He wasn't going to touch that one for anything. "She's female," Mike said. "She's programmed for that."

Uh-oh, Tom thought. *Now Mike's in major trouble.*

"What?" Elizabeth gasped, resting her palms on the table.

Tom held her arm. He could tell she was on the verge of jumping to her feet.

"I'm sure Mike knows it's hard for everyone," Tom said, trying to defuse the situation. "But women *are* socially conditioned for marriage through images in the media and so on. Men, on the other hand, are always portrayed as trying to avoid marriage."

"And that makes it all right?" Elizabeth retorted angrily.

"Of course not," Tom said. He looked over at Mike and gave him an exaggerated nod. "Right, Mike?" Tom barely resisted the urge to kick him under the table.

"Uh, sure," Mike agreed. "But right or wrong, look at Steven."

"I hope you're not saying that's my fault," Billie hissed, her face turning a deep shade of purple.

Elizabeth reached out to touch her hand. "It's nobody's fault."

"Yes, it is," Billie snarled, yanking her hand away. "It's Steven's fault."

Jessica glared at Billie, her blue-green eyes starting to smolder. "My brother is under a lot of pressure."

Elizabeth jumped up and leaned over her sister. "So is Billie."

Billie pulled Elizabeth back down. "You can stop defending me, Liz," she snapped. "I'm quite capable of that myself."

Tom watched in horror as one member of their party after another hurled angry words. He was starting to get indigestion and he hadn't even eaten yet.

Steven sat at the table in Alfredo's restaurant, trying to remain calm. For the past half hour he'd been doing his best to stay out of the arguments swirling around him. But he was fed up with everyone talking about *him* and *his* motives.

"May I say something, please?" he asked quietly. No one seemed to hear him speak.

"Wait a minute, Mike," Jessica was saying loudly. "If you think that Steven—"

It was no use. There was only one way to get this group's attention. "Enough!" Steven shouted, slamming his fist down onto the table. Water sloshed out of glasses and a knife clattered to the floor. The table went totally silent.

"The prophet speaks," Billie said.

Steven glared at her. "Don't make me any madder than I already am."

"*Me* make *you* mad?" Billie snorted. "I thought that was impossible. I thought nobody could make anybody anything. Weren't those your words?"

Steven bit down on his lower lip. That's what he'd said, all right. And it might have worked if everyone around him wasn't so aggravating.

"I was trying to help us," Steven said between clenched teeth. "Studies show one out of every two marriages ends in divorce. I didn't want that to happen to us."

"So you chose to hide your head in the sand?

You think ostriches have happier home lives?"

"If that's what it would take for us to stay together, then yes," Steven explained. "I would have hid my head in the sand. But I didn't expect you to come and peck at me while I was doing it."

"I wasn't pecking at you!" Billie screamed. "I was trying to get some help."

"Well, I was *trying* to help," he snarled. "Don't you know there are a thousand things that can go wrong in a marriage? One false move and the whole ship goes down."

"So you wouldn't make any moves at all," Billie snapped. "How's that supposed to help?"

"It kept us from fighting, didn't it?"

"I'd rather fight than live with some kind of spaced-out, self-help robot," Billie shouted.

"If you keep screaming at me, maybe you won't have to!"

"Billie. Steven," Elizabeth said, reaching out to Steven's arm.

Steven felt a hand on his sleeve pulling at him, and he realized he was standing up. So was Billie. The other people in the restaurant had stopped eating and were staring at them. Their waiter hovered in the background with a tray of food, obviously afraid to bring it over. *This is crazy*, he thought. *I've got to get a grip.* Even if he wasn't going to follow those self-help books to the letter, he didn't have to make a scene.

"I think we should leave, Billie," Steven said in a calmer voice.

"I think you're right." Billie looked embarrassed too. "We're tired. We need sleep more than we need food."

"Sorry, guys," Steven said. He stepped away from the table. Nobody said anything or tried to stop them, and he realized they were probably just as glad to see him go as he was to leave.

Bruce took a long sip from his foamy cappuccino and glanced around the charming outdoor café where he and Lila were sitting. It was a warm, still night, but as his eyes rested on Lila he realized she was shivering in her thin beige summer dress. "Are you cold?"

Lila shook her head and toyed with her untouched espresso. "It's hard for me to relax with the law offices of Ballard, Smythe, Loeb & Hobbs looming above us."

Bruce looked across the street at the white marble facade of the law firm's building. Maybe coming to Gigi's Café hadn't been the smartest idea. But they made the best coffee drinks in town and served a great goat cheese salad.

"I keep thinking our lawyers are going to come out and start screaming at us."

Bruce grimaced. He hadn't thought of that. He shook his head. "They'd never do that to a client." *But then who would have expected them to get so violent with each other?* he wondered.

Lila sighed. "And to think I felt stupid that we couldn't come to an agreement. At least *we* were fighting over our own money. Though I kind of wish we didn't have to fight over anything."

Bruce nodded. "Lila, I've been thinking about that, too." He leaned across the wrought-iron table and gingerly took her slender hand. "Maybe

191

it's premature for us to be discussing marriage. It's not that I don't want us to get married one day," he explained, "but all this fighting over our pre-engagement prenuptial agreement has made me see that this isn't the right time."

Lila smiled and squeezed his hand back. "I agree. If this is what getting engaged is about, I'm willing to wait."

Bruce pushed his chair closer to hers and let out a big sigh of relief. "Good. I'll call the lawyers in the morning and tell them the contract is off. We'll postpone the legal side. But what do you say about practicing the kissing side?"

Lila winked. "I say pucker up, sweetheart."

Bruce laughed and hugged her tight. *Lawyers or no lawyers,* he thought, *kissing is one thing we can always agree on.*

"I'm glad we left," Billie said, taking Steven's arm as they walked across Alfredo's parking lot to their car. "I don't think I could have eaten anyway." *Not with the way my stomach is feeling,* she thought. It was one big knot, even though she and Steven had managed a mutual apology in the foyer of the restaurant.

"I second that," Steven said, opening the passenger door for her. "As soon as my head hits the pillow I'm going to be out for the count."

Billie got in and leaned against the headrest. "Not until you've written your vows," she reminded him tiredly. She would be so glad when this was over.

Steven groaned. "I'm exhausted." He turned the key in the car's ignition.

Billie closed her eyes. *Why are you doing this to me?* she thought. "Steven, I'm serious. Don't even think about going to sleep until you've written those vows." She'd die of embarrassment if they stood in front of the minister tomorrow and Steven had nothing to say.

"Okay, okay," Steven muttered. "I'll write them."

Billie sighed. Her wedding day was supposed to be the happiest day of her life, but so far everything leading up to it had been a total nightmare.

"Whew," Mike said as he watched Steven and Billie drive off from his window seat in the restaurant. "Let's hope they calm down."

"I'm sure they will," Jessica snapped, "with proper apologies."

Mike looked over at her. Was she still mad about that ball-and-chain comment he'd made? Talk about sensitive.

As the waiter served their food Elizabeth pointed to Steven and Billie's plates. "Can you wrap those up, please? I'm afraid two of our party have left."

"As if he didn't know," Mike mumbled to himself. The whole restaurant had watched them leave. *But better they work out their differences now,* he thought. Marriage wasn't easy. He had his memory of those stormy weeks with Jessica to thank for that lesson.

Mike twirled his fork around his linguine and clam sauce. He took his first bite. Delicious. *And so is that pair of legs walking toward me,* he thought. He followed the curve of the woman's body until his eyes reached her face. "Gina." He smiled broadly. "How are you doing?"

"Mike!" Gina exclaimed. "What a treat to see you." She bent down and gave him a soft kiss on the cheek.

Mike jumped up.

"Mike." Jessica frowned. "Where are you going?" There was an edge to her voice, but he chose to ignore it.

"I'll be right back." He was going to walk Gina over to her table. "Here by yourself?" he asked as he and Gina made their way past the old-fashioned cherry-wood bar to the other end of the dining room.

"I wish I was now," Gina said. "Then you could be joining me. But actually, I'm meeting my fiancé." She took her seat, crossing her long shapely legs.

Mike clutched his chest. "Ouch. Don't tell me another good-looking woman is settling down."

"Afraid so." She giggled. Her laughter tinkled just as he'd remembered it.

Mike felt a tap on his shoulder and turned, half expecting Gina's fiancé. Instead he came face-to-face with Jessica, her skin a boiling scarlet red.

"Jess," Mike said, "this is Gina, an old friend of mine."

"She doesn't look very old." Jessica sniffed. "And from the way you ran over here, I'd say she's a lot more than a friend." She turned and flounced back toward their table.

"Sorry, Mike—I hope you're not in trouble," Gina teased. "Don't tell me another good-looking man is settling down."

Mike shrugged. "Jessica has an overactive imagination sometimes. But I'd better go."

Gina took his hand. "Too bad whatever she's thinking isn't true."

Mike smiled. He'd always liked Gina. But as long as he was with Jessica, he didn't want to be with anybody else.

He got as far as the bar when out of nowhere Jessica pounced on him.

"How dare you embarrass me like that," she snarled.

"What?" Mike asked, feeling a flash of annoyance. "All I did was say hello to an old girlfriend. Come on, let's go back to the table. Our food is getting cold."

"You should have thought about that before going off to flirt with some other woman," Jessica scoffed, standing firm.

Mike sighed and leaned against the cool surface of the polished counter. "You want to have it out here instead of in front of your sister and Tom? Fine. I haven't seen Gina in a long time and I'm glad I ran into her. I don't ignore people." Maybe that ball-and-chain remark hadn't been so wrong after all. If it was up to Jessica, he'd probably be on a leash.

"There's a difference between being polite and being Don Juan," Jessica raged.

"You're the one who told me to be myself," Mike shot back. Now he was getting mad. "Well, that's me. You can't have it both ways."

"I want you to be yourself around me," Jessica cried. "Not around all the other women in the world!"

Mike groaned. "I'm either being the Mike that attracts you or I'm not. If I am, then it attracts other women too."

Jessica pushed away from the bar. "That's the most arrogant, self-centered statement I've ever heard," she screamed, her aquamarine eyes glaring at him furiously.

Mike spread his hands. "I can't change chemistry. You either take it or you leave it."

"Then I leave it!" Jessica turned on her heels and stormed out of the restaurant.

Mike groaned and went back to the table. "I'm afraid there's another meal for the doggie bag." He pointed to Jessica's plate. He sat down, took a bite of his ice-cold linguine and clam sauce, and changed his mind. "I guess I'm out of here too."

"It looks like it's just you and me, sweetheart," Tom said in his Humphrey Bogart accent.

Elizabeth laughed. Tom's Bogie was almost as good as his Aunt Sylvia. She pushed away her plate and looked down the long empty table. Full doggie bags were waiting at three of the places. Mike had managed a few bites before he left, so there was one half-eaten plate. "Not much of a rehearsal dinner. But we have enough food left over to feed us for a week."

"If only we were back at SVU," Tom said. "This sure beats the cafeteria."

The waiter appeared at the head of the table. "Can I get you anything else?" he asked. His face was inscrutable. Elizabeth could only guess what he must have thought of all the comings and goings at their table.

196

"Do you mind if we hang around a little while, Tom?" She wasn't ready to get back to her parents' house yet. Who knew what battles were still being waged there?

"Not at all," Tom said. "We'll have two coffees, please."

The waiter nodded and walked away.

"I'm going to try Aunt Sylvia one more time," Elizabeth said, pushing her chair from the table.

"Are you sure you want to do that?" Tom asked. "We've been having such a nice time."

Elizabeth raised an eyebrow. "You call this a nice time? The whole dinner has been one disaster after another."

"I mean between you and me," Tom said. "Forget about the rest of the inmates. I don't want you to get upset about Aunt Sylvia all over again."

Elizabeth leaned over and kissed him. "I promise I won't. But I'd feel guilty if I didn't try her once more."

Tom shrugged. "Fair enough."

Elizabeth crossed the elegant mirrored hallway connecting the restaurant to the hotel. An elderly man was using the lobby phone. He stood with his back to her.

Elizabeth walked over and perched on the armrest of a plush blue velvet chair and looked around the almost empty lobby. *Not much activity here,* she thought. A bellboy pushed his luggage trolley toward the elevator, followed by a weary-looking couple with cameras slung around their necks. "Certainly no Aunt Sylvia," she said with a sigh.

Elizabeth looked back at the man on the phone.

His faded tweed jacket seemed somehow familiar. It reminded her of something a professor in an old movie would wear, with its comfortable worn look and gray corduroy patches at the elbows. She could almost smell the pipe smoke.

No, Elizabeth thought, *there's something else about that coat.* She shook her head. The man sure was talking up a storm. She was just about to give up and go back to the restaurant when the man hung up the phone. Elizabeth took a step forward. At the same time the man turned and their eyes met.

Elizabeth let out a terrible scream. This wasn't her imagination. The man before her didn't just look like Uncle Howard—he *was* Uncle Howard. She was standing face-to-face with a dead man! The last thing she remembered was the carpeted floor coming up to meet her.

"Hold on, Liz," Tom called as he raced across the hotel lobby. "I'm coming." He'd heard her scream from all the way inside the restaurant.

By the time he got there a small crowd had gathered. Elizabeth was sitting up on the royal blue carpeted floor. Tom stopped dead in his tracks. The man patting her hand and speaking to her looked just like Uncle Howard! No wonder Elizabeth had screamed. Tom dropped to one knee beside her and began pushing the man away.

"It's okay, Tom," Elizabeth said, smiling weakly. "This is Carl Lister, a friend of Aunt Sylvia's."

Tom could only stare at the man in shock. "Oh yeah. Then why did he kidnap her?"

"No one has kidnapped me, young man," a spry voice said. Tom turned to find a bright-eyed woman with gray hair before him. Even without the cat-eye glasses, there was no doubt about it—this was Aunt Sylvia. Tom would know her anywhere.

"Aunt Sylvia." He laughed. "You have no idea how relieved I am to finally meet you."

A few minutes later the four of them were seated around their rehearsal dinner table in Alfredo's, four cups of steaming coffee in front of them. The old picture of Aunt Sylvia and Uncle Howard lay in the center of the table.

"I didn't mean to give you such a fright, child," Aunt Sylvia said. "I left word at your mother's house with a young man named Marcus. I told him Carl would be picking me up at the airport and not to worry about me."

Elizabeth groaned. "Marcus. That's the caterer who disappeared without a forwarding address. No wonder we never got the message."

"I'm so sorry," Aunt Sylvia said. "I should have called again, but of course it never occurred to me that you'd think something so dreadful had happened."

Tom smiled. *It's called an overactive imagination,* he thought. That policeman in Santa Carmine had been right.

"But where have you been?" Elizabeth asked. "And your telegram said you were arriving with Uncle Howard."

Aunt Sylvia dabbed at her eyes with her napkin. "As you know, your uncle Howard is dead."

"We knew that," Tom said. "We were afraid you didn't."

"Don't be daft, young man. I may be old, but I'm not senile."

Tom blushed and mentally kicked himself under the table.

Elizabeth picked up the photo from the center of the table. "But why is Mr. Lister in this old picture?" she asked.

"I'm getting to that, dear." Aunt Sylvia stirred two sugar cubes into her coffee. "Carl; his wife, Miriam; your uncle Howard; and I all grew up together. Carl and Miriam were childhood sweethearts and so were Uncle Howard and I."

"So it was taken on a joint holiday," Tom prompted.

"You are an impatient young man," Aunt Sylvia scolded.

"Sorry." Tom blushed. But the suspense was killing him.

"We were on holiday," Aunt Sylvia continued. "Every few years when we could manage it, the four of us would get together at the shore. That's where we got married, in a double wedding."

"That's so romantic." Elizabeth sighed, her blue-green eyes shining.

"Yes, it was." Aunt Sylvia smiled. "Anyway, that picture," she said, looking at the one of herself and Carl Lister, "is a good forty years old. We were celebrating our fifteenth wedding anniversary that year."

Wow, Tom thought, *I wasn't even alive then.*

"The sad part is," Aunt Sylvia continued, "it was the last time we were all together. Uncle Howard's health started to deteriorate soon after."

"And Miriam and I moved to Anchorage," Mr. Lister added. He looked over at Aunt Sylvia. "So much time has passed."

Elizabeth poured a drop of milk into her coffee. "What made you get together now?"

"Was Santa Carmine the town where you had your reunions?" Tom asked.

"Such inquisitive young people," Aunt Sylvia said to Mr. Lister. "I guess we'd better start at the beginning." She paused and took a sip of her coffee.

Tom settled more comfortably into his chair. This was his favorite part of being a journalist— when all the bits and pieces finally came together.

"As I told you," Aunt Sylvia said, "Uncle Howard and I, and Carl and Miriam, got married in a double wedding. This was right at the start of World War II."

"Howard and I were being shipped out the next week," Mr. Lister said. "Nineteen forty-one. I remember it like it was yesterday."

Tom nodded. His grandfather had been at Pearl Harbor.

"In those days if you had a sweetheart, you got married quick. No one knew if they'd make it back," Mr. Lister added.

"Luckily Howard and Carl did." Aunt Sylvia dabbed at her eyes again. "That was the happiest day of my life. After my wedding day, of course."

"But why did you say you were bringing Uncle Howard?" Elizabeth asked.

Yeah, Tom wondered. Aunt Sylvia seemed normal

enough, but that Uncle Howard telegram had been pretty weird.

"Just before the boys went off to war . . . ," Aunt Sylvia started. She turned to Tom. "They were just boys then, like you are, young man."

Tom gulped. War. That would sure make you grow up fast.

"Anyway," Aunt Sylvia continued, "the boys didn't know whether they'd make it back alive or not."

"We made wills," Mr. Lister said. "We wanted our ashes sprinkled in the ocean where we'd been having such a good time during our honeymoon."

Tom crossed his arms and nodded his head. "Santa Carmine." Another piece of the puzzle locked into place.

"That's right," Aunt Sylvia said, this time not scolding him for jumping in. "I've had Uncle Howard's ashes in a little urn on the mantelpiece above my fireplace for many years. I've been holding on to them, thinking that when I died, our ashes could be sprinkled in the ocean together."

"But then I called," Mr. Lister said. "My wife, Miriam, passed away last year. I'd been sorting through some papers and came across Sylvia's number, and I called her."

Aunt Sylvia took Mr. Lister's hand. "I'm so glad you did." She turned to Tom and Elizabeth. "We'd been out of touch for such a long time."

"I was lucky you didn't move," Mr. Lister said tenderly.

Tom looked over at Elizabeth. Now she was dabbing her eyes.

"We decided to sprinkle Howard and Miriam's ashes at the same time," Aunt Sylvia said. "So when I telegrammed that I was coming with Uncle Howard, I meant I was coming with his ashes."

"Oh, I get it," Tom said. No wonder.

"We realized it would probably be the last chance for the four of us to be together," Aunt Sylvia said.

"That's a beautiful story." Elizabeth sighed. "I'm so glad you two found each other again."

"And I'm going to keep it that way," Mr. Lister said. "Life's too short to let loved ones slip away."

Tom squeezed Elizabeth's hand. He'd learned that lesson himself. He would never let Elizabeth slip away.

Steven knocked softly at his parents' bedroom door. "You'll have to do better than that," he told himself. "Or they'll never hear you." He knew his mother and father were sound asleep. They'd called it a night at nine thirty, and it already was past eleven.

"Dad," he said to the closed door, knocking louder. "I have to talk to you." Steven had been carrying what felt like a hundred-pound weight on his back all evening. If he didn't share it with someone soon, it was going to flatten him like a pancake.

Steven heard a noise. It sounded like a muffled moan. Could it have been, "Come in"?

He hoped so. He gave the bedroom door a tentative push. "Dad?" he said again, poking his head in. The lights were out, but there was no snoring. A good sign. It meant his father was awake.

"Dad?" Steven said one last time.

"I'll be right there," his father's voice came back in a harsh whisper. "Don't wake your mother."

Mr. Wakefield padded over in bare feet.

"I . . . ," Steven began to say.

His father motioned for silence by putting a finger to his lips. Mr. Wakefield stepped out into the hallway in a pair of rumpled blue-and-green-striped pajamas and closed the bedroom door behind them. "I hope this is important. You almost woke up your mother."

Steven took a deep breath, twisting in his hand the bottom of the T-shirt he wore over his sweatpants. It was important, all right. It was the most important thing he could imagine. "I didn't write my vows."

Mr. Wakefield groaned. "Is that all, Steven?" He reached for the doorknob.

Steven panicked. "No," he said quickly, putting his hand against the door. "I didn't write my vows because I *couldn't* write them."

Mr. Wakefield rubbed some sleep from his eyes. "So you need some help?"

Steven shook his head. "I don't mean I *can't* write them. I just *couldn't* write them."

Mr. Wakefield made a face. "Steven, you're not making any sense."

Steven's eyes darted around frantically. He knew he wasn't making sense. But that was because what he had to say was so difficult to admit. "I can't write them." Steven hesitated, his eyes finally settling on his father's big toe. "Because I don't want to."

"Steven," Mr. Wakefield said sternly, "no one else is going to do it for you."

"I don't want to write them," Steven said, gathering up all his courage and looking his father straight in the face, "because I don't want to get married!"

Chapter Eleven

"Steven, just calm down," Mr. Wakefield said. "Everyone has prewedding jitters." They were standing in the Wakefields' living room. His father had insisted they come down to hash things out.

Steven crossed his arms and leaned against the wall beside the fireplace. He realized he'd been swinging his arms wildly as he spoke. He didn't want his father to think he'd cracked up altogether, but his mind was whirling frantically.

"It's more than prewedding jitters," he said with a groan, crossing the room and flopping down onto the couch. "I have a million questions and no answers."

"Everyone feels that way," Mr. Wakefield said, taking a seat on the ottoman. "That's what prewedding jitters are all about."

Steven shook his head roughly. "This is different," he insisted. "I must have read ten books over the past two days, and I still don't know anything more than I did before. Marriage is a major mystery to me."

"Marriage is more like an art than a science," Mr. Wakefield said. "It's not something you can read about and then neatly categorize. Nobody has all the answers going in."

"But I don't have *any* of the answers," Steven protested. His mind had become so muddled, he couldn't even remember why he and Billie were getting married.

"Marriage is organic. It grows and changes as you and your partner grow and change."

"But what if we grow and change separately?" Steven asked. "What if one morning we wake up and don't even recognize each other?" He knew it sounded far-fetched, but what if one morning Billie turned out to be a stranger?

"That's where the work comes in," Mr. Wakefield said. "You'll both change. That's guaranteed. The trick is to change into people you both like."

Steven dropped his head into his hands. How could he guarantee that? "I don't understand any of this. Why can't we just go on the way we've been?"

Mr. Wakefield put a hand on Steven's shoulder. "You can't be expected to figure this all out before you're married. The answers come as you need them."

Steven looked up. "But what if I don't like the answers?" he cried. "What if it turns out this was all wrong and Billie and I are one of the fifty percent who don't make it?"

Mr. Wakefield shook his head slowly. "I can't answer that, Steven. Nobody can. That's the chance you have to take. But with hard work—"

"It seems like such a big risk," Steven moaned, interrupting his father. He didn't want a lecture on the hardship of marriage. He wanted some enlightenment on what it was all about.

Mr. Wakefield shook his head again. "If you're thinking of calling off the wedding because you don't have all the answers, I think you're making a mistake. But it's getting late now." He looked up at the wall clock over the fireplace. "And you're obviously very tired. I think you should sleep on it. See how you feel in the morning."

"But I'm getting married in the morning," Steven mumbled, getting up and following his father upstairs. He would try to sleep on it. It was true that things always looked better in the morning. *They'd better,* he thought, *because they can't look any more confusing than they do right now.*

Jessica threw her fashion magazine straight across her bedroom. "I can't believe Mike McAllery," she scoffed. She'd been all ready for bed, dressed in her favorite pink silk teddy and matching tap pants, when a major-league case of insomnia had hit. She'd hoped that a quick turn through *Vogue* would help take her mind off Mike and the ugly scene between them at Alfredo's Restaurant. But even high couture couldn't hold her interest now. She rolled over on the tangled mass of sheets on her bed and hid her face in her pillow.

This is ridiculous, she thought, jumping up and

beginning to pace around her thick green carpet. Was it too much to ask for Mike to behave himself when they were out in public?

"But you didn't like it when Mike acted all clean cut and innocent either, Jess," she reminded herself. And it was true. She'd accused him of acting more like a brother than a date when he'd been on his good behavior. She'd even gone so far as to tell Mike to be himself. "But did he have to throw my words back in my face like that?" she moaned.

Jessica leaned her head against the cool surface of the full-length mirror on the back of her door. "So what am I supposed to do?" she asked herself miserably. She liked the real Mike, but it was maddening that the rest of the female population did too. She threw herself back down on her bed. *I'll never get to sleep now,* she thought wretchedly.

A sudden *rat-tat-tat,* like heavy raindrops, brought her to the window. "It can't be raining," she murmured, pushing back the ivory pleats of her bedroom curtain. It had been a clear, beautiful evening. She looked up at the dark night sky. Bright stars twinkled back at her. She jumped as another series of sharp pings clattered against the glass. She looked down. It was Mike, flinging gravel at her window.

"Mike," Jessica called, opening her window. "Stop that! You'll wake up the whole house." The guest bedroom was just next door. Aunt Matilda and Uncle Clifford waking up was the last thing she needed.

Mike let the gravel fall from his hand. "Can we go for a ride?" he asked. She didn't see his bike, but two helmets were at his feet.

"I'm in my pajamas," Jessica said, sulking. "I've already gone to bed."

"Please," Mike said. "We need to talk."

Jessica hesitated. She had the arguments on the tip of her tongue. *There's nothing to talk about. You obviously don't understand me,* went one of them. *Why should I, after the way you acted tonight?* went another. But Mike was right. It was time they talked.

Jessica leaned out of the window. "Okay, Mike. Give me a minute to change."

The wedding music had just started. Billie turned this way and that, searching for her long white wedding veil, but the room was totally empty.

Mrs. Wakefield rushed in, her arms filled with wilted pink-and-purple flowers. "You'll have to wear these as your veil," she said, weaving the hideous flowers through Billie's hair.

Billie pushed her away and started to run down a long empty corridor that seemed to stretch out forever. The music was swelling, and she covered her ears to block out its roar. Suddenly she was inside a church. But all the pews on the bride's side were empty.

"Where are my parents?" she screamed. All the faces from the groom's side turned to her and began to laugh. They pointed at her dress. Billie looked down and gasped. Her wedding gown was full of holes.

Steven stood by the altar chanting, "You will obey me, you will obey me."

"Where am I?" she cried. Billie lurched forward in the long narrow cot set up in Elizabeth's bedroom

211

with a loud scream. She looked around frantically as her eyes grew accustomed to the dark. Her heart was pounding and her whole body was drenched. She felt as if the ceiling had opened up and a bucket of cold water had been poured on her.

Steven's house, she thought, trying to calm the intense hammering in her chest. *I'm in Elizabeth's room. I'm getting married tomorrow.* But that didn't help at all. Instead her heart pounded even harder. "I'm getting married?" she cried.

It wasn't just a bad dream! *No,* she thought, *most of my nightmare is true.* Her parents really weren't going to be at her wedding. And her wedding dress really had been ruined, though luckily Val had created a satin sash to cover the worst of the stain. "What am I going to do?"

Billie jumped out of bed and wrapped one of Elizabeth's terry-cloth robes tightly around her. *I've got to do something,* she thought. She walked down the hall to Mr. and Mrs. Wakefield's bedroom. Her hands were shaking, but somehow she steadied them long enough to knock on the door.

Mr. Wakefield opened it as if he'd been waiting there.

"I've got to talk to you," Billie said, her bottom lip trembling.

He nodded for her to go on.

She tried, but her voice was closing up. She was shaking so hard she was afraid she'd fall to pieces. "I . . . ," she began, faltering. "I . . . ," she started again, forcing herself with all her nerve and courage to say the words. "I . . . don't want to get married."

212

Mr. Wakefield swayed on his feet. "Wait here." He put his hands on her shoulders and placed her against the wall. Only then did she realize she was about to fall.

Mr. Wakefield crossed the hall and knocked loudly on Steven's bedroom door until he appeared. "Look," he said, taking Steven's arm and leading him over to Billie, "I'm not going to be up all night because the two of you are having prewedding jitters. I want you to go downstairs to the kitchen, make a big pot of coffee, and talk to *each other* until you work this out."

Billie looked at Steven. *Is he having doubts too?*

"My father's right," Steven said, trembling himself. "We should talk."

Billie slipped her hand into his. If Steven was also having second thoughts, then maybe her attack of nerves was completely normal. *On the other hand,* she thought, *maybe it means we should call off the wedding.*

"I don't know what you want from me, Jess," Mike said. They were sitting close together on the beach, barely touching. He could feel her shivering in her heavy college sweatshirt and blue jeans, even with his motorcycle jacket wrapped around her shoulders. He wanted to hold her and warm her, but she'd already made it clear she was there just to talk.

"I don't know either," Jessica said, making figures in the sand with a stick.

He watched as she drew a heart, his chest giving a lurch as she rubbed it out with her palm.

Mike looked around the empty beach. The surf was gentle, and the moon, hanging high in the velvety blue sky, was bright. A romantic night. But there was nothing romantic going on between them now. He turned back to her. "I act one way and you tell me not to. I act another way and you get mad. I don't know what to do. You're giving me mixed signals."

Jessica sighed and looked up at him. He could so easily lose himself in her beautiful aquamarine eyes.

"I can't help it," she said. "I'm confused myself. I don't want you to change, but I can't cope with you the way you are."

Mike rubbed his arms up and down across his thin T-shirt. Without his jacket he was getting cold himself.

"I see you with those other girls," Jessica went on. "The way they look at you, the way you look at them. It makes me miserable."

"It doesn't have to be that way," Mike said. "It could be just you and me. Nobody else."

"But that was too intense," Jessica said, exhaling deeply.

Mike shook his head. He didn't know what to do. Everything he suggested, she struck down. "I don't know what to say, Jess. Except that I'll always love you. And if you can figure out what you want from me, I'll do my best to give it to you. But you've got to tell me what that is because it's got me beat."

Jessica nodded. One silent tear dropped onto her sneaker.

"Hey," Mike said softly, cupping her face. "No crying. You don't want your eyes all puffy for your brother's wedding." He gently pulled her to her feet. "Come on, I'm taking you home. I don't need an answer now. You sleep on it and let me know."

Jessica unlocked the front door of her parents' house and slipped silently inside. The house was quiet as a tomb. It was just like old times at Sweet Valley High—sneaking in after curfew. She winced at the noisy creaking of the hinges. Even that hadn't changed. She turned and was softly closing the door behind her when she felt someone on the other side begin pushing against it.

Jessica froze. She'd heard about burglars who pushed in behind a victim as they were returning home.

"Jess," came the familiar voice of her twin sister. "Let me in."

"Liz?" Jessica said, opening the door. Elizabeth was the last person she'd expected, even with all the cracks she'd made about a midnight rendezvous between her sister and Tom. "What are you doing up at this hour?"

"It's a long story," Elizabeth said.

Jessica smirked as she locked the door behind them. She could imagine the punch line.

"It's not what you think," Elizabeth said firmly. "I was having a long talk with Aunt Sylvia and her friend Carl Lister. They practically had to throw us out of Alfredo's."

"I didn't know Aunt Sylvia was coming with a date."

215

"Like I said," Elizabeth replied, "it's a *long* story."

Jessica shrugged. She had enough on her mind without worrying about the dating habits of their ancient aunt. "I guess everyone is in now. I'm going to turn out the light in the living room."

Jessica walked over to the Chinese lamp on the low coffee table by the couch. She was just about to switch it off when the sound of heavy snoring stopped her. Her father was fast asleep in his easy chair, his head lolling on his chest.

"Liz," Jessica called in a whisper. "Dad's in here sleeping."

Elizabeth joined her at the foot of his chair. "We better wake him."

Jessica reached down and touched her father's shoulder.

"What? What?" he asked, still half asleep. "Talk to each other."

"Dad," Jessica said, "are you all right?"

Mr. Wakefield blinked and looked around the room. "I must have fallen asleep."

"I'll say," Elizabeth said. "How long have you been down here?"

Mr. Wakefield looked at the clock above the mantelpiece. "Not more than fifteen minutes." He yawned. "First your brother woke me up and then a half hour later Billie needed to talk."

How odd, Jessica thought. Weren't the wedding preparations finished? "Why?"

"Steven and Billie seem to be having some doubts about getting married," Mr. Wakefield said. "Unfortunately both of them decided they needed advice from the old pro." He let out another long yawn.

216

Jessica couldn't believe it. Steven and Billie's wedding was less than a few hours away. "And I thought I was having trouble with my feelings toward Mike." She sighed to herself. "This is double trouble."

"What did they decide?" Elizabeth asked.

"I don't know," Mr. Wakefield said. "I sent them to the kitchen with stern orders to talk it out."

"Are they still in there?"

Jessica didn't bother to wait for an answer. She would see for herself. She started toward the kitchen.

"Slow down," Elizabeth said, catching up to her. "Let's just peek."

Mr. Wakefield was close on their heels.

Jessica softly pushed open the door. Steven and Billie were in the kitchen, all right. Sound asleep with their heads on the table. Their hands, though, were joined in the center.

Jessica closed the door quietly so as not to wake them. "Is it on or off?" she whispered.

Elizabeth and her father shrugged.

"We'll have to wait until tomorrow," Mr. Wakefield said. "Now let's get some sleep."

Elizabeth nodded and headed for the stairs. But Jessica held back. She had her own demons to wrestle tonight. And as usual, they involved Mike McAllery.

Steven's head shot up from the kitchen table as his mother burst in.

"It's ten o'clock," she screamed, all vestiges of her sanity gone. "I overslept. Preheat the oven, throw in the canapés."

217

Elizabeth and Jessica stepped into the kitchen, both in their pajamas and rubbing sleep from their eyes.

Mrs. Wakefield turned on them. "Elizabeth," she shouted, "put the linen on the tables outside and then set them with the good silverware. Jessica, arrange the chairs in front of the pulpit and lay down the bridal carpet. Steven, Billie, take your showers and get dressed." She clapped. "Hurry, hurry," she said. "The wedding is at eleven thirty!"

Steven felt as if he'd been hit by a tidal wave. He could hardly catch his breath. He turned to Billie, gasping. She was cowering in the far reaches of the kitchen. Her face was drained of color. How would they ever get it all done in an hour and a half?

But wait a minute, Steven thought. He reached for Billie's hand. Hadn't they worked this out last night? Billie had been feeling just as much trepidation as he had. *There's not going to be a wedding,* he thought. *We called it off!*

Steven let out a deep sigh of relief. They weren't getting married. He didn't have to worry about these wedding preparations anymore. Nobody did. *But I still have to tell my mother!* He gulped as he realized the pain he was about to inflict.

Steven shuddered. His mother had run from the room, but he could still hear her barking orders. What was he going to say to her? The image of a firing squad flitted across his mind. How could he tell her after all the work she'd put into this wedding? He couldn't. *I'll join the foreign legion,* he thought. It sounded drastic, but it was the only way out.

*　　　*　　　*

As Billie sat trembling at the Wakefields' kitchen table, she could hear Mrs. Wakefield barging around the other rooms in the house. Steven's firm, reassuring hand was the only thing keeping her grounded. How could they tell Mrs. Wakefield that the wedding was off? Just thinking about it sent shivers down her spine.

Mrs. Wakefield bounded back into the kitchen, making both Billie and Steven jump. "Why are you two still sitting here?" she shrieked. "You have to shower and you'll need at least half an hour to get dressed. And Billie, you have your makeup and hair to worry about."

Billie turned to Steven. "Tell her," she urged.

"Tell me what?" Mrs. Wakefield asked.

Steven's face turned white, and he shook his head furiously.

"What?" Mrs. Wakefield demanded, turning to Billie.

"Nothing," Billie squeaked. She couldn't find the nerve either.

Mrs. Wakefield flew from the room.

Billie looked back at Steven. "You've got to tell her."

"I can't." Steven moaned. "I can't face her."

"Then what are we going to do?" Billie asked, her bottom lip quivering.

"I'm running away from home," Steven said, getting up from his seat.

Billie grabbed his arm, pulling him back down. "Don't be ridiculous. You can't run away from home. You don't even live here."

"You tell her," Steven stated, his jaw set. "It'll

be easier coming from you. She wouldn't murder someone she wasn't related to by blood."

Billie could just imagine herself walking up to a frantic Mrs. Wakefield, tapping her on the shoulder, and saying, "Oh, by the way, you know this wedding you've been running around like a madwoman planning? It's off." The idea was so frightening, Billie hid her face in her arms. "I can't," she sobbed. "It's too terrifying."

Steven jumped up. "My dad! We'll get him to do it."

Billie ran after Steven to find Mr. Wakefield. He'd understand. He'd told them to talk it out in the first place. And they had. They'd realized they loved each other, but they weren't ready to tie the knot yet. *He* could tell Mrs. Wakefield. After all, it had been practically his idea.

Mr. Wakefield stood outside his bedroom, his arms crossed. "No," he said emphatically. "Married or not, you're both grown-ups. You were mature enough to start this wedding ball rolling, so it's time to be mature enough to stop it."

"But it's going to crush her," Steven wailed.

Mr. Wakefield shook his head. "It's up to you and Billie to tell your mother. I suggest you hurry up. Waiting will only make matters worse." He went back into his bedroom, closing the door with a resounding thud.

Billie and Steven turned to each other and groaned in unison.

"We could pull straws," Billie suggested.

"I always lose at that," Steven complained. "And I can't promise I'd do it anyway."

Billie searched frantically in her mind for a solution. If she and Steven couldn't do it and Mr. Wakefield wouldn't, what were they going to do? "Maybe we *should* run away."

Steven made a face.

Just at that moment Elizabeth came walking past them, heading for the shower.

"Elizabeth!" they both screamed.

Elizabeth backed against the wall. "What? Do you need to get in there first?"

Billie took one arm, Steven took the other, and they led her back into her bedroom.

"It's a matter of life or death," Steven said.

Billie nodded firmly. "Life or death," she echoed.

Steven took a deep breath. "We're not getting married and we need you to tell Mom." He exhaled.

Elizabeth dropped onto her bed. "That *is* life or death," she gasped.

Billie stared at Elizabeth, pleading with her eyes. "Please," she begged. "We both tried, but it was no good. We don't have the nerve."

Elizabeth looked from Billie to Steven to Billie again. "Okay," she said with a sigh. "But you guys owe me big time."

Chapter Twelve

Elizabeth found her mother on the back patio, staring distractedly at a circle of chairs. Elizabeth had taken a quick shower before coming to talk to her. She'd needed a dose of cold water to get her brain cells working. *This,* she thought, *is going to be a delicate matter.*

"Mom," Elizabeth said tentatively.

Mrs. Wakefield turned to her, a few loose wisps of hair spilling out of her bun. She looked like a woman with more on her mind than she could handle. "I can't decide whether the jazz musicians should sit here or farther back." She pointed to a few feet away, near the geranium bushes.

Elizabeth gulped. It didn't matter where they sat now. And it was up to her to break the bad news. In the shower she had thought of a hundred different ways she could approach her mother. But in the end she'd decided straightforward and honest was the best. She took a deep breath. "Steven and Billie have decided not to get married," she blurted.

Her mother reeled, and Elizabeth grabbed her arm, leading her the few steps to a chair.

"You can't be serious," Mrs. Wakefield gasped, her face a ghostly pale.

"I'm afraid I am," Elizabeth said gently, reaching for a glass from one of the tables and then frantically looking around for something cool. She spied a bottle of Perrier in an ice chest and poured her mother a drink. "They were up most of the night talking and realized they weren't ready."

Mrs. Wakefield took a distracted sip, spilling some on her blouse. She looked around the backyard. "You mean all this work and there's no wedding?"

Elizabeth patted her mother's hand. It was breaking her heart to see her mother looking so sad. *If only there was something I could do,* Elizabeth thought. "We can still have a party," she ventured.

Mrs. Wakefield shook her head despondently. "It's not the same. A wedding is a celebration of a couple's love. There's nothing to celebrate now."

Elizabeth nodded. *It's true,* she thought. With no wedding, a party would be a sad affair.

The doorbell rang, jolting them both.

"Oh no," Mrs. Wakefield cried. "The guests are arriving already. You get it, Liz, I can't face anyone yet. I'm going up to my room for a good cry."

"No, don't, Mom," Elizabeth said, jumping to her feet. "Let me get the door and I'll be right back." She couldn't let her mother go off feeling like that.

224

Elizabeth rushed to the door. Aunt Sylvia and Carl Lister were standing on the threshold. Aunt Sylvia was wearing a long cream-colored dress. In her hand was a soft hat covered with a matching veil. Mr. Lister was in a tux.

"Hello, dear," Aunt Sylvia said. "I hope we're not late. We had to run all over town this morning to get our own wedding clothes. Carl and I decided last night that as soon as your brother's wedding is over, we'd go down to the justice of the peace in Sweet Valley and get married ourselves."

"Congratulations!" Elizabeth exclaimed, giving them each a big hug. "But I'm afraid there's not going to be a wedding here. Steven and Billie have called it off."

"Oh, dear," Aunt Sylvia said. "That's so sad. Your poor mother."

Wait a minute, Elizabeth thought, a huge grin crossing her face. Why couldn't they have a wedding anyway?

"Your timing couldn't be better," she said. "Come in. Mom is in the backyard. I have great news for everybody."

Elizabeth led them back to the patio, where Mrs. Wakefield was putting a cold compress on her forehead.

"Mom," Elizabeth said, "it's Aunt Sylvia and her new fiancé, Carl Lister. They were going to get married by the justice of the peace this afternoon. But under the circumstances I think we should have their wedding right *here*."

"Oh, Elizabeth," Mrs. Wakefield cried, jumping up, "what a great idea!"

Elizabeth turned to Aunt Sylvia and her soon-to-be uncle Carl. "Is it all right with you two?"

The tears in both their eyes were answer enough.

"I always dreamed of a wedding surrounded by family," Aunt Sylvia said. "When Uncle Howard and I, and Carl and Miriam, got married, there were just the four of us. This is the most lovely wedding surprise we could have imagined."

Elizabeth blinked back a few tears of her own. This day was going to have a happy ending after all.

Aunt Sylvia's heart skipped a beat as the wedding march began. She clung to Tom's arm as he escorted her down the aisle. She felt like she was eighteen years old again. Carl smiled at her from the altar.

This is just lovely, she thought, looking around. All these smiling young people. And so many relatives, too. She hadn't seen some of them in ages. And they'd done such a wonderful job with the wedding preparations. Small tables dotted the patio around the glistening blue pool. The fragrant aroma of white tulips and yellow roses scented the air. Gaily colored streamers and Chinese lanterns had been strung across the yard. In the airy white tent an enormous buffet had been laid out. *It's like a dream come true.*

She squeezed Elizabeth's hand as she got up to the altar. Her beautiful maid of honor wore a delicate silk dress of sky blue. Elizabeth had given her that photo of her and Carl in a silver frame. *Something old.*

226

Aunt Sylvia turned to look out at the crowd. She waved at Billie. Such a nice young girl. Billie had given her a white wedding purse. *Something new.*

She waved to Alice, her niece, whose hard work had made this wonderful wedding possible. She'd lent Aunt Sylvia a beautiful ruby broach. *Something borrowed.*

And she smiled at Jessica, who'd given her a lovely ribbon to put on her hat. *Something blue.*

"Dearly beloved," the minister began, "we are gathered here today . . ."

Aunt Sylvia smiled. *Such a lovely family,* she thought. *I must remember to visit them more often.*

Jessica pressed her body close to Mike's, swaying to the lilting jazz rhythm that floated across the Wakefields' backyard. Every movement made the sequins on her gold lamé dress shimmer in the bright afternoon sun. She sighed deeply. Mike looked even more fantastic than usual today in his sharply tailored blue designer suit. His crisp white collarless shirt set off the finely sculpted features of his face and accentuated his healthy, bronzed skin. Being in his powerful arms almost made her forget what she had to say to him. *But I have to,* she reminded herself.

When the band stopped playing, she took his hand and led him behind some shrubbery at the side of the yard. There was a garden bench there and they sat together, their knees pressing.

Jessica looked deep into Mike's golden eyes. She still wasn't sure if this was what she wanted to do.

But for now, she thought, *it's the right thing.*

"Mike," she said, looking away. "I thought a lot about last night and I have an answer for you."

He pulled back a little, as if already sensing it was bad news.

Jessica's heart started to pound. There was no going back now. "I love you," she said. "But—"

"You don't have to say it," Mike interrupted. "It's over between us."

Jessica shook her head slowly. "I'm not saying that. Maybe someday we can be together again."

Mike turned away and stared off toward the grassy path they'd walked down. "But not now," he murmured.

"No," Jessica whispered. "I've realized I've been trying to grow up too fast. I've been skipping steps. Being in business with Val. Being with you. I need to go back to the beginning. I need to finish school and do a million other things, too."

Mike sat motionless. Jessica wasn't even sure how much he'd heard. Should she try again? Should she tell him that like a career, a love like theirs was something she hoped to have someday? But that she needed to wait until the time was right? Would that make more sense to him?

Mike looked up and took her hand. He smiled faintly, but there was sadness in his eyes. "You sound like you're growing up already, Jess. I'll clear out of your life after the reception. When you're ready, *if* you're ready, you know where you can find me. Anytime."

Jessica leaned forward, her eyes damp. Mike reached out, and she melted into his arms. She closed her eyes as their lips met and she lost herself in a last dizzying kiss.

Mike was the first to break away. "We'd better get back to the party," he said hoarsely.

Jessica nodded, but she couldn't seem to will her legs to walk away from him. Her hand found his. She closed her eyes, sadly realizing that this might be the last time they would be together. Then she felt Mike's hand slowly slip away from hers. When she opened her eyes, he was gone.

"What a beautiful wedding," Lila murmured in Bruce's ear as he led her around the dance floor. Her purple satin skirt whirled after her. The Wakefields' aunt and new uncle made such a happy couple. "Just think, that could have been us."

Bruce gave a start and held her slightly away. "Are you serious?" he asked. His handsome tanned face lost a little of its glow.

Lila laughed. "Just a little," she said, smiling at him. "The rest of me is glad we came to our senses."

"Whew," Bruce said, pulling her back toward him. "I thought you might have been bitten by the wedding bug."

"You mean by the same bug that bit you?" Lila asked, raising one eyebrow. "Didn't I see you dabbing at your eyes when Uncle Carl lifted the veil and kissed Aunt Sylvia?"

Bruce blushed. "It was a piece of dust. I had to get it out of my eye."

Lila grinned. "You're just a big softie and you know it."

"Okay," Bruce said, twirling her around. "I give up. Weddings have that effect on me too."

"But I'm still glad we came to our senses," Lila said.

"Me too," Bruce agreed. "We learned our lesson. Trying to jump into marriage or even a pre-engagement prenuptial agreement before you're ready just makes everyone unhappy."

"That's for sure." Lila sighed. She looked over Bruce's shoulder at Billie and Steven. They were holding hands and laughing. They certainly were a lot happier now. "Even Billie and Steven weren't ready for marriage, and they've been together a lot longer than we have."

Bruce nodded. "I'm really glad their decision not to get married didn't bust them up."

"And I'm glad our decision to wait hasn't hurt us," Lila said, wrapping her tawny arms around Bruce's neck. "We can love each other without taking such a serious step."

"I know they say the happiest day of a girl's life is supposed to be her wedding day." Billie giggled, adjusting the loose strap of the emerald green cocktail dress Elizabeth had lent her. "But would it sound very silly to say my happiest day is my non-wedding day?"

Steven, dressed in his rented tux, laughed and pulled her toward him under the white tent. "Under the circumstances, not at all. But I've been thinking. Even though it's our nonwedding day, I still have some vows I'd like to make."

Billie looked up from his shoulder, her eyes wid-

230

ening. "Really? I didn't think you'd gotten around to writing those."

"I didn't write them." He smiled. "These are promises I don't need to struggle over. They've come to me naturally."

Billie frowned. She wasn't sure what he was getting at.

Steven stood straighter and took her hand. "I, Steven Wakefield," he said solemnly, "promise to come and visit Billie Winkler in Spain next semester while she's wowing the Spaniards with her musical genius."

"Oh, I get it." Billie laughed, entwining her fingers in his. She could do this too. "I, Billie Winkler, promise to welcome Steven Wakefield with open arms when he comes to visit me in Spain. And to look forward only to the times we're together and try not to get too upset over the times we're apart."

Steven nodded. "I agree with that too. And I promise not to feel threatened by the separation and to write every day."

Billie's dark blue eyes sparkled happily. "I promise to call once a week."

Steven smiled. "I promise to lighten up in my approach to life."

Billie laughed and kissed his nose. "I thought you were only doing easy promises."

Steven grinned and pulled her close again, wrapping his arm around her shoulders. "That's easy to promise because I want us to be happy."

"Okay," Billie agreed. "Then I have one too. I promise to keep my feet on the ground, even though my head may be in the clouds."

Steven laughed. "Now who's making the hard promises?"

"Like you said, I want us to be happy too."

"Should we shake on it?" Steven asked.

"I think a kiss would be better, don't you?" Billie teased. "Even the nongroom and nonbride are entitled to that."

"Gather around everybody—Aunt Sylvia is going to throw the bouquet now," Mrs. Wakefield announced.

Aunt Sylvia watched as Aunts Eloise, Matilda, and Agnes herded the young unmarried women into a group before her. *Such reluctance in the young things,* she thought. *Must be their natural shyness.* She could remember at their age how she and her friends would become positively frenzied when it was time for the bouquet to be thrown. Everyone jostled to get a place in the front.

"Dears," Aunt Sylvia said, "you'd better stand closer. I can't throw that far."

She spied Aunt Agnes pushing a reluctant Elizabeth and Jessica up to the front row. "That's right," Aunt Sylvia murmured to herself. She'd aim in that direction. She liked both the young men her nieces were seeing.

"Now where's Billie?" Aunt Sylvia asked. She wasn't going to throw it until Billie was there.

Aunt Matilda marched Billie up to the front between the twins. She seemed to be fighting Aunt Matilda.

"And those other young girls," Aunt Sylvia said, "don't forget them." Aunt Eloise was practically grabbing that friend of Jessica's with the long brown hair. *Lila*, she thought, *that's her name.* Aunt Sylvia had seen her dancing close to a handsome young man. They seemed to be in love. "And bring those other young women closer," Aunt Sylvia said. *All those young women looked so in love when they were with their boyfriends,* she thought. *What's gotten into them now?*

"Okay, Aunt Sylvia," Mrs. Wakefield said. "Everybody's ready. You can throw the bouquet."

Aunt Sylvia turned so her back was toward the crowd. She lowered the bouquet of tiny snowdrop roses before her and then flung it as hard as she could over her head. She turned to see which of the lucky girls would catch it. But to her shock, girls and boys alike had scattered. The lovely bouquet landed with a thud on the patio.

"My word," Aunt Sylvia said to Carl. "The way they acted, you'd think I was throwing a stink bomb."

"I guess these young ones just aren't in the marrying mind yet," Carl said.

"Hmmm," Aunt Sylvia said, watching as the young people paired off again on the dance floor. "I guess you're right, Carl. After all, why should they be in any hurry? They have all the time in the world."

Everyone who reads Elizabeth's journalism paper is dead! And now she's afraid she's next. Find out if Elizabeth makes it in the next Sweet Valley University Thriller, **RUNNING FOR HER LIFE.**

SIGN UP FOR THE SWEET VALLEY HIGH® FAN CLUB!

Hey, girls! Get all the gossip on Sweet Valley High's® most popular teenagers when you join our fantastic Fan Club! As a member, you'll get all of this really cool stuff:

- Membership Card with your own personal Fan Club ID number
- A Sweet Valley High® Secret Treasure Box
- Sweet Valley High® Stationery
- Official Fan Club Pencil (for secret note writing!)
- Three Bookmarks
- A "Members Only" Door Hanger
- Two Skeins of J. & P. Coats® Embroidery Floss with flower barrette instruction leaflet
- Two editions of *The Oracle* newsletter
- Plus exclusive Sweet Valley High® product offers, special savings, contests, and much more!

Be the first to find out what Jessica & Elizabeth Wakefield are up to by joining the Sweet Valley High® Fan Club for the one-year membership fee of only $6.25 each for U.S. residents, $8.25 for Canadian residents (U.S. currency). Includes shipping & handling.

Send a check or money order (do not send cash) made payable to "Sweet Valley High® Fan Club" along with this form to:

SWEET VALLEY HIGH® FAN CLUB, BOX 3919-B, SCHAUMBURG, IL 60168-3919

NAME _____
(Please print clearly)

ADDRESS _____

CITY_____ STATE _____ ZIP_____
(Required)

AGE _____ BIRTHDAY_____ /_____ /_____

Offer good while supplies last. Allow 6-8 weeks after check clearance for delivery. Addresses without ZIP codes cannot be honored. Offer good in USA & Canada only. Void where prohibited by law.
©1993 by Francine Pascal   LCI-1383-123